Prairie Pearl

THE STORY OF ELLEN STOVER

Arleen Brenner

© Copyright 2004, Arleen Brenner.
All rights reserved.

No part of this publication may be reproduced, stored in a retrieval system, or
transmitted, in any form or by any means, electronic, mechanical, photocopying,
recording, or otherwise, without the written prior permission of the author.

Note for Librarians: a cataloguing record for this book that includes Dewey Decimal
Classification and US Library of Congress numbers is available from the National
Library of Canada. The complete cataloguing record can be obtained from the
National Library's online database at:
www.nlc-bnc.ca/amicus/index-e.html
ISBN 1-4120-4281-X
Printed in Victoria, BC, Canada

TRAFFORD

Offices in Canada, USA, Ireland, UK and Spain
This book was published *on-demand* in cooperation with Trafford Publishing.
On-demand publishing is a unique process and service of making a book available
for retail sale to the public taking advantage of on-demand manufacturing and
Internet marketing. On-demand publishing includes promotions, retail sales,
manufacturing, order fulfilment, accounting and collecting
royalties on behalf of the author.
Book sales in Europe:
Trafford Publishing (UK) Ltd., Enterprise House, Wistaston Road Business Centre,
Wistaston Road, Crewe CW2 7RP UNITED KINGDOM
phone 01270 251 396 (local rate 0845 230 9601)
facsimile 01270 254 983; info.uk@trafford.com
Book sales for North America and international:
Trafford Publishing, 6E–2333 Government St.,
Victoria, BC V8T 4P4 CANADA
phone 250 383 6864 (toll-free 1 888 232 4444)
fax 250 383 6804; email to bookstore@trafford.com

www.trafford.com/robots/04-2088.html

10 9 8 7 6 5 4 3 2

Prairie Pearl has been written in memory of my grandparents and great grandparents who were some of the first pioneers to settle in Saskatchewan.

It is a tribute to my mother who was born in Canada and orphaned at a very young age. It is also a tribute to my father who immigrated to Canada at the age of eight.

A special thanks goes to my daughter and editor, Cynthia Reitenbach. Thank you Amanda Reitenbach, my granddaughter, for gracing the cover of this book with your beautiful smile.

God has blessed us all!

Introduction

PRAIRIE PEARL is a work of fiction. Any of the characters in the book that may resemble real people is purely coincidental. To my knowledge there has never been a town named Pearl in the province of Saskatchewan in Canada.

The real developers of the Canadian West were the hardworking pioneers that tilled the soil and built the roads, railroads and other structures that set the pace for the great life that we enjoy on the prairies today.

History is often written by the rich and powerful people of the times. Women played a very vital role yet they were only considered as chattels having few or no rights.

Young girls were especially enslaved in their surroundings. They were often married in their early teens to men old enough to be their fathers.

There were a few exceptions. When a man cherishes his wife, he also instills great qualities in his children. Henry Stover was just that man.

His daughter Ellen becomes a true leader as she learns to think and reason at a very young age. Ellen's mother taught her the meaning of being a true Christian.

There is a time for humour in the lives of these hard-working people. Without a laugh or two their lives would have been unbearable.

Tough times call for tough solutions. Ellen is well prepared for such times. Take a walk back in time to the year 1920 when Ellen, as a ten-year-old girl, begins her story.

Chapter 1

I WILL NEVER forget the day that Amy arrived. It was a beautiful quiet Saturday in August of 1920, but there was nothing beautiful or quiet about Amy. She was all beaten and bruised when I answered the door. She was sobbing and blood was running down her face.

"I need to see your mother," Amy said.

"Mother," I called. "Amy is here and wants to see you."

"Be right there."

Amy was trembling and sobbing so hard that I started to shake along with her. I was just ten years old.

"Mother," I called again. "She needs you right away."

Mother came scurrying to the door, "My God Amy, what has happened to you?"

"My father has thrown me out of the house," Amy choked.

"Ellen, go to your room and close the door please."

"Yes, Mother," I replied.

I knew that I had to go, as I was never allowed to question my parents' wishes. I gladly went to my room to get away from the terrified look on Amy's face. What had happened to her?

Amy went to the same one room schoolhouse as I did. She just completed grade eight. It was the last school year for most students, as the boys were needed to work on the farm or in their father's business. The girls were expected to get married and move on to a life of their own.

Mother soon called me and said that I should go outside and play, as Amy needed to rest.

Then Mother headed to the barnyard where Father was repairing a fence. I was soon watching a hummingbird dart back and forth in the nasturtiums. The hummingbird was my favourite bird. They were so tiny and their wings fluttered so rapidly. They always seemed to be moving. I tried to follow the bird to find its nest but it was just too fast for me.

Amy's face kept coming back to my mind. Her blue eyes always sparkled but today they were filled with pain. They should have been like an ocean of blue made deeper by her checkered dress in its many shades of blue. Her dress was torn in several places. My stomach got a funny feeling. Who would do this to her? Why?

I was glad when Mother called me to set the table for supper.

"Is Amy all right?" I asked.

"She will be fine," Mother replied. "Now wash your hands

and set the table."

We went to Pearl every Saturday night. Only about fifty people lived in Pearl. My parents would shop for food and supplies and I would play with my friends in the schoolyard. Sometimes we would all go and visit one of the families that lived in town.

Father came in and was washing in the porch when Amy came to the kitchen. Mother had given her a dress that was too large for her but it was neat and tidy. Amy's golden hair was brushed away from her face exposing a swollen black eye.

We all gathered at the kitchen table and Father gave the blessing and asked for help for Amy in getting her life back together. A tear rolled down Amy's cheek.

"Henry, would you mind going to town with Ellen tonight? I think I will stay home with Amy," Mother said as she passed the bowl of potatoes to me.

"Do you have a list of things that we need?" Father asked.

"Yes. We only need a few groceries."

After supper on Saturdays, we always had a bath before going to town. Father and I carried in the big metal bathtub from the porch. Mother had a large pot of water heating on the wood stove for our baths. We all shared the same bath water; I was always the first one in the tub then Mother and then Father. Mother would just add hot water as it was needed.

Tonight was different. I bathed first and then Father. I said

9

good-bye to Mother and Amy, Father kissed Mother good-bye and we headed for the door.

"Bye, Amy," Father said.

"Good-bye Mr. Stover. Good-bye Ellen."

"You will feel much better after a nice warm bath. I will put my lilac bath salts in the water," Mother said.

"Thank you, Mrs. Stover."

Father hitched the horses to the buggy and we got in and headed for Pearl. Father handed me the reins and told me to hold on to them without moving them. They were made of leather and pretty heavy for me.

"How do you get the horses to stop?" I asked.

"Pull both reins tightly. Try it."

I pulled the reins but I pulled the right one harder and the horses started to turn to the right. Father took the reins and guided the horses back to the center of the road.

"You must pull both reins with the same strength," Father said. "Now, try it again."

I took the reins and this time I was able to stop the horses.

"Very good, Ellen."

Soon we were in town and Father dropped me off at the schoolyard. I ran to meet my friend Sarah. I told her about Amy coming to our house.

Sarah was quick to reply, "Amy's father beat her and sent her away."

"But why?" I asked. "Why would her father beat her?"

"I think she disobeyed the priest," Sarah replied.

10

We were not Catholics, but I knew that no one ever questioned the priest. His word was law. Sarah and I joined some other girls who were playing on the swings.

I saw Father go into the doctor's office. I wondered why he was going there. I hoped he wasn't sick.

Pearl's doctor was simply known as Doc. I never heard him called by any other name. He often made house calls in the country when he was called. His office in Pearl was in his home where he could be found when he wasn't away on a house call.

"Ellen, come push me," Sarah called.

My thoughts returned to Sarah and the playground. I went behind her and placed my hands on the ropes. I pulled them back and let them go. I then pushed the board that she was sitting on until she was swinging pretty high. I sat on the next swing and placed my hands on the ropes. I kicked the ground to get myself started and then I pumped my legs back and forth to get the swing to go higher. It was a good feeling. The gentle breeze ruffled my bangs as I swung back and forth.

We played on the swings until Father came with the buggy. We usually stayed in town till almost dark, but tonight Father was ready to leave very early. We only lived a mile away from Pearl so it took less than fifteen minutes to make the journey.

"Can't we stay longer?" I asked. "I'm having so much fun with Sarah."

"Not tonight Ellen. We need to go home and spend the

rest of the evening with Mother and Amy. Come along now."

I slowly boarded the buggy with a helping hand from Father.

"Bye, Sarah. See you at church tomorrow."

"Bye, Mr. Stover."

"A good evening to you young lady," my father responded.

The evening was calm. The clouds were small tonight. I loved to watch the clouds, as they seemed to have many stories to tell. I didn't know where they went when the sky was clear. Did they go to some far away place like British Columbia or maybe the United States of America? What did they see? What great secrets did they hold? I told the clouds all my secrets and they kept them for me. They never told a soul. They were like a best friend.

I fell asleep in the buggy on the way home and Father carried me off to bed. I woke up once and I could hear Mother and Father talking in low voices in the kitchen. They would be sitting in the dark holding hands as they often did in troubled times. I could not hear what they were saying but I was sure they were discussing Amy. They would solve her problems. Somehow they always came up with the solution. With that in mind I drifted back to sleep.

Sunday was a day of rest and a time to be thankful for the many good things that we had. As we prepared to go to church, Mother asked Amy if she would join us. She said she would. Mother had stayed up late the night before to mend and wash Amy's dress.

Amy came from a Catholic home and we were headed to a little Lutheran church in the country.

Father brought the horses and buggy to the door. Church had always been the center of our lives. We met every Sunday and a lot of social functions were planned with the congregation. Father dropped us off at the door and we proceeded to enter the church. The organist was playing my favorite hymn. *Oh, come, come, come, come; Come to the church in the Wildwood, Oh come to the church in the dale,* I sang to myself. I spotted Sarah on my right.

"Hello, Sarah," I said.

"I can't talk to you," she replied as she walked away.

My mother took my hand and gently squeezed it urging me to move forward.

"Why can't Sarah talk to me?"

"We must forgive, forget and move on," my mother replied.

My mother used this expression when she didn't want to reply to a question. It was her way of saying that the subject was not open for discussion.

We headed for the third pew from the front on the left. Mother urged Amy to take a seat at the end of the pew. Amy was walking with her head bent. A tear trickled down her cheek and she quickly brushed it away. I sat down beside Amy and Mother took her seat beside me.

I looked around for Sarah and the rest of the Millers. They were sitting near the back of the church.

"Why aren't the Millers sitting in the pew in front of us

like they always do?" I whispered to my mother.

"The church is open to everyone. It is their choice where they want to sit," Mother said.

Father joined us and he and Mother exchanged that look that only they understood.

They bowed their heads in prayer and I said a prayer of my own.

Please God, make Sarah talk to me. I don't know why she won't. Bless Mother and Father and help Amy. Amen.

The sermon seemed to be so very long today and I was restless in my seat. Most of the talk was too much for me to understand anyway.

After church was over, it was customary for everyone to shake the pastor's hand and then stand around and visit with friends and neighbours.

My father introduced Amy to the pastor. His response was, "Yes, I know Amy." He did not shake her hand.

"Nice to see you, Henry, Mary and Ellen," he said as he quickly shook our hands.

We moved to the bottom of the steps and Mother approached Mrs. Black who coordinated the church's quilting bees, "Will we be meeting at your house on Tuesday?"

"Oh, I've had to cancel it this week," Mrs. Black replied as she quickly moved away and called out to another lady.

Mother loved to quilt and she looked forward to the quilting bees. The ladies would gather at someone's home and they would all work on a quilt together. They would hand stitch the layers of cloth and wool together. Some of the quilts were really nice and colourful; they were often made with many small pieces of cloth.

They were called patchwork quilts. Most of the patches were made from garments that children had outgrown or worn out. There were still parts of the garments that were usable. The rest of the cloth was used for rags.

I needed to go to the toilet before we left for home. The church had two small toilets that we called outhouses, one for the women and one for the men. When I was finished, I used a sheet from the Eaton's catalogue to wipe myself and then I threw it down the hole. As I was getting ready to leave, I could hear someone coming.

"Will I see you Tuesday at the quilting bee?" one asked.

"I heard Emma tell Mary that it had been cancelled," the other replied.

"Well, we can't be associating with people that keep company with a little prostitute," came the reply.

I did not know what a prostitute was. I opened the door and quickly ran to my parents who were already loaded in the buggy.

"What's a prostute?" I asked.

Mother and Father exchanged that look again.

"We must forgive, forget and move on," my mother replied. "Now hop up here and join us."

"Why are we leaving so soon?" I asked.

"We are all tired and need to get some rest," Mother responded.

Amy was silent all the way home. She sat with her head bent. I could only wish that she would smile and show her nice straight white teeth. Amy was such a pretty girl.

The boys at school were always trying to get her attention, but she would give them little or no response. At school Amy often took a book outdoors and sat and read in the shade of a big maple tree. She was an honour student. At her age Amy was expected to be thinking about marriage and raising her own family.

The buggy ride seemed to take forever. I looked up to the sky for some solace. It was a nice sunny day and a few clouds floated slowly by. I dreamed of floating on one of them. The cloud would be so soft and fluffy like it had hundreds of feather pillows joined together. Amy could come with me and have her troubles drift away into the wide blue yonder. The clouds lived in the heavens where everything was so peaceful and quiet. There were no troubles in heaven. The clouds looked after everyone's problems and that's how heaven was free of all the sorrows that people faced on earth. A white cloud seemed to stop in the sky.

Do not worry, Ellen. Everything will be fine. Have faith.

Suddenly I felt really tired. My eyes started to droop and my head felt heavy. Amy put her arm around my shoulder and hugged me to her.

I fell asleep wondering if I could believe in my song. *No spot is so dear to my childhood, as the little brown church in the vale.*

A special cloud quieted me. *Sleep, Ellen, sleep. I will take care of you.*

Chapter 2

AMY STANFORD was a hard worker and Mother was grateful to have her. She was helping Mother can vegetables from the garden. Today we were gathering cabbage heads to make sauerkraut. Mother cut the cabbage head away from the stock of the plant, I carried the cabbage head to the house and Amy dug the remainder of the cabbage stock out of the ground and put it in a cart that Father had brought to the garden.

"Have you ever helped make sauerkraut, Amy?" Mother asked.

"Yes."

Amy remained silent and only responded if she was asked a question. She looked so sad. I tried to talk to her about school but she did not seem interested. I spotted some butterflies and started chasing them around the garden. Mother had to call me several times to remind me that I had cabbage to carry. It was more fun chasing butterflies. We had a large veranda with an old kitchen table and four chairs. It was used for many things. Today we would be processing the cabbage there. I had put most of the cabbage on the table and when it was full, I piled the heads in a large circular metal basin on the floor.

When we were done gathering the cabbage, we took a break and had a glass of milk and some coffee cake. Mother referred to the cake as kuchen which is the German word for cake. She got the recipe from an elderly German lady that lived in Pearl. Kuchen was made with a sweet bun dough on the bottom. It was topped with fruit like apples, raspberries, saskatoons or rhubarb. A crumb topping made with flour, brown sugar, cinnamon, butter and vanilla was sprinkled on top of the fruit. The German lady told Mother that the secret to good kuchen was a bun dough that was thin enough to pour and vanilla in the crumb topping.

Today we were having saskatoon kuchen. Mother and I had picked the berries earlier in the spring and she had canned them for later use. The berries grew wild on small shrubs on the farm. It was delicious but my favorite kuchen had apples on top.

After our break Mother started shredding the cabbage. Amy removed the hard core from the center of the cabbage and cut the heads in half. Amy continued to core and slice as Mother shredded the cabbage. She used a shredder that Father had made. It had two cutting blades that were mounted in a wooden frame. The tool was about two feet long and a foot wide and it could be placed over the top of a twenty-gallon crock.

Mother would put the cabbage inside a square wooden frame and slide it back and forth over the blades shredding the cabbage as she went. When there was a layer of cabbage on the bottom of the crock she would sprinkle coarse salt over the cabbage. She would then place several whole cabbage heads in the crock. These heads had the cores removed as well. After that, she would continue to shred cabbage and pack it firmly around the heads. When she had covered the heads with a thick layer of cabbage, she would salt it again. Layers of full heads and shredded cabbage would be added until the crock was full. Mother worked most of the day to fill the crock.

Just as Mother finished making the sauerkraut, Father came to the house. He had been out in the field on the binder harvesting his wheat. The binder was a machine that gathered the grain and tied it in bundles that were called sheaves.

"That was good timing, Henry," Mother said. "We just finished."

Father and Mother carried the crock into the porch where it would be left to ferment.

Mother placed a wooden board directly on the shredded cabbage. She then placed a large stone that weighed about twenty pounds on the board. The crock was covered with a clean white cloth. It would take approximately ten to fourteen days for the cabbage to turn to sauerkraut. The process was a stinky one and we were always glad when the crock was moved to the root cellar for storage. We often chanted a phrase: *Sauerkraut, sauerkraut, stinky in, stinky out.*

Amy looked very tired. I wondered about her troubles.

What could she have done that was so terrible? Did the priest not forgive, forget and move on?

We all had supper and Father was ready to return to the field to continue running the binder until dark. Mother made a sandwich to send with him and filled a quart sealer with coffee. Mother poured the hot beverage into the glass jar with sugar and cream and then it was wrapped in a towel to keep it warm.

Mother, Amy and I returned to the garden where we picked tomatoes. Most of the tomatoes were still green but they had to be picked early because it would soon turn cold at night and the tomatoes would freeze and be spoiled. Mother and Amy made green tomato pickles that would be put in the cellar for use in the winter. I hated green tomato pickles. Some of the green tomatoes were put in the cellar as well. When they were placed in a cool dark place, it slowed the ripening process. Others were put near a window in the porch so that they would ripen faster in the warmth of the sun.

We returned to the garden to check for cucumbers. Shortly after we started picking them, Amy collapsed.

"Ellen, get your father!" Mother yelled. There was great urgency in her voice.

I ran as fast as I could.

"Father," I yelled. "Mother needs you. Something is wrong with Amy."

Father stopped the horses and shouted, "Go back to the house!" He unhitched the horses and ran past me as he headed toward the house. He was hitching the team to the buggy when I got home.

"Get in the buggy, Ellen. We have to get the doctor."

He had carried Amy to the veranda before I got there. Now, he gently picked her up and took her into the house. There was blood on her dress.

Suddenly, I was very frightened. The doctor was never called unless it was a matter of life and death. What was wrong with Amy?

We were off to Pearl with Father urging the horses to go faster and faster. It was very scary to be riding this fast in the buggy. I wanted to ask what was wrong with Amy, but Father was concentrating very hard on handling the horses.

"When we get to the doctor's office, I need you to stay with the horses. Just hold the reins steady."

At the doctor's office Father jumped off the buggy, handed

21

me the reins and ran inside. I had to sit quietly with the reins as I did not want the horses to move. I wasn't sure if I could control them.

Doc came running out of his office with his black bag. He boarded his own buggy and was soon heading for the farm. Father took the reins from me and we headed over to Main Street.

He tied the team to a hitching post and we were soon walking down the sidewalk.

"Let's go in the café and have a little treat," Father said.

That was very unusual as there was never any time wasted during harvest.

"Can I have an orange pop?"

"Sure."

"Can I have a coffee with cream and sugar and an orange pop for the young lady?" Father asked the waitress.

"Coming right up."

She served us and moved away quickly and busied herself behind the counter. There was no one else in the café at the time.

"What's wrong with Amy?" I asked. "Will she be all right?"

"I'm sure Doc will look after her."

I knew that Amy had a serious problem, as the doctor was called. My parents were very money conscious and it cost money to see the doctor.

"Are you anxious to go back to school?" Father asked.

22

School would start sometime in September. It seemed like a long time yet.

"I think so."

"What do you like best about school?"

"I love math and reading books."

"What is your favourite book?"

"*The Tortoise and the Hare*. I like *Aesop's Fables* because they always have a moral to the story."

"Yes, and they are good stories too. I think it's time for us to head for home."

We had finished our beverages so Father went to the counter to pay the bill. We left the café and boarded the buggy. Father drove very slowly. As we neared our house, we could see the doctor leaving and heading our way. We met in the lane and both men tipped their hats and continued on their way.

When we got home, I rushed into the house.

"How is Amy?"

"She will be fine but she needs to rest. You must be quiet Ellen."

I went outside and sat on the step. Something had to be very wrong. Why was she bleeding? Father went inside and he and Mother spoke in whispers. I could not hear what they were saying.

Soon Father came outside. "I'm going back to the field. See you later, little lady with the mystic blue eyes," he said.

"Bye Father."

The sky was clouding in. I looked for a friendly one but they all seemed to be dark and troubled. It was the same in my world.

But the clouds live in heaven. They live in peace and harmony.

There was a break in the cloud formation and the sun came through. Then my friendly cloud appeared.

Be patient Ellen. Be patient. All will be fine.

Amy remained in her room for two days, and I was only allowed to go to her door and talk to her for a little while each day. Our conversations did not tell me what was wrong with Amy.

The week came to an end. It was Saturday. I was looking forward to going into town.

"Will Amy be coming to town with us tonight?" I asked at the supper table.

My father replied, "We'd love to have her come. Will you come with us Amy?"

"I'd rather not," she said. "You go ahead and I'll clean up the kitchen."

"Thank you, Amy," Mother said. "That is very thoughtful of you."

Mother, Father and I had our baths and dressed for our trip to town. Soon we were in the buggy and headed for Pearl. Our first stop would be at the general store where Mother wanted to buy some material for dresses. Father dropped us off at the store and drove off to tie up the hors-

24

es. A neighbour of ours was leaving the store as we were entering.

"Hello Libby," Mother said.

Libby looked the other way and quickly moved away.

In the store Mr. Eastman said hello to us and moved on to help another customer. We went straight to the yard goods, and Mother started choosing the material she wanted. I wandered around the store, as there was so much to see. The store sold food, dry goods and small hardware items. I guess that's why it was called a general store; it generally had many things. Mother found the material she liked and was waiting for Mr. Eastman to cut it for her. He seemed to be too busy with other customers. Mother set the bolts aside and picked up the other things that she needed and went to pay for them. Mr. Eastman came to the counter.

"I need some cloth," Mother said.

He cut the material and as Mother was paying for her purchases Father came in the store to collect us.

"Hello John. How are things with you?" Father asked Mr. Eastman.

Mr. Eastman just grunted and went to the storage room at the back of the store.

"I guess that's about it," my father said. "I think we should head for home."

"But I want to go to the playground to play with the other kids," I said.

25

"Another time Ellen."

I was not happy but I had no other choice but to hop into the buggy and head for home. The sun had set and stars would soon twinkle in the sky. The clouds had moved away. There would be no one to share my thoughts with.

When we returned home, Amy was sitting at the kitchen table reading a book. She had lit the kerosene lamp to provide the light for her to read. We did not stay up late, as it was costly to run the lamp. We got up early when the sun rose around five in the morning. That was a way to use the natural light at no cost.

Amy had cleaned up the supper dishes and swept the kitchen floor. Everything looked neat and tidy. Mother thanked her for doing such a good job.

Mother served coffee and kuchen. Amy and I had a glass of milk. Mother made such good cakes. She had topped this one with raspberries from the garden.

The crumb topping was so delicious. I asked for another helping.

"I guess it's all right just this one time. Would you like another piece Amy?"

"Yes, thank you. It is very good."

Soon we were getting ready for bed, as we would be going to church the next day. Amy asked if she could stay home from church. Mother insisted that she go.

"We don't ask much of you Amy. But you must go to church. You should always have a place to go in troubled times. Stay in touch with the Lord. He will see you through your trials."

I heard Amy crying in her room as I tried to fall asleep. I went to the window to search for a cloud. There were several moving in to darken the star spattered sky. They looked like rain clouds. They did not offer me their usual comfort.

There are troubling times ahead, Ellen! Be prepared!

I returned to bed and tried to sleep. Amy had stopped crying and silence filled the air. A streak of lightning flashed in the distance followed by a rumble of thunder. I hated storms at night. The darkness made it so much harder to endure. Mother said that it was very important that we have lightning as it revitalized the soil with nitrogen. The thunder shook the ground and made openings in it so that the rain could soak in and wash down to the roots of the plants. Without the lightning, the thunder and the rain we would not be able to grow our crops. I tried to hold onto that good thought to make the oncoming storm a pleasant adventure.

The storm was moving in rapidly now and the sky was alight with lightning. More thunder boomed and then the rain came. It poured very hard for a few minutes and then it just stopped. I was glad as I was tired and needed to go to sleep.

I returned to the window one more time and spotted the last cloud moving to the east.

Good-bye Ellen. See you soon. Be strong! Be strong!

Chapter 3

AMY WAS up and preparing breakfast when I came to the kitchen. She was making bacon and eggs, fried potatoes and toast. She had a pot of coffee on the stove for Mother and Father. She and I would have milk. Amy had buttered the toast with butter that Mother and I had made earlier that week. We made the butter by putting cream in a wooden container that was circular with a turning handle on it. It was spill proof and we turned the handle for over an hour. When we were finished, the cream had formed little globs of butter and the liquid remaining was buttermilk. Mother would strain the butter and add salt to it. She would bottle the buttermilk. Father loved to drink it and Mother used it for baking. The butter was placed in a four sided wooden frame that formed it into a rectangular shape that weighed about a pound. We usually made about two pounds at a time in the summer and more in the winter because we had an ice house to store it.

"Good morning Ellen. Would you set the table for me?"

"Sure. I'm starved."

I put the dishes on the table along with saskatoon jam, raspberry jam, a red tomato relish and salt and pepper. Mother and I had picked the berries and she had made the jams and relish. Most of our food was grown and processed at home.

Mother and Father came in from the barn where they had been milking the cows. Father carried a fresh pail of milk.

"Something smells good," Mother said. "Oh, Amy, thank you for making breakfast. What a nice surprise."

"You're welcome," Amy replied as a faint smile appeared on her face.

Mother and Father washed up in the porch and came to the table. Father said grace asking for the food to be blessed and for guidance in the days ahead. Amy served breakfast and we all ate ravenously.

Soon we were having a pleasant buggy ride to church. We had left early so that we could enjoy the outside air. Our summers were short and sometimes fall could be very cold. The sky was clear blue and naked. There wasn't a cloud to be seen. The sun was shining brightly but it was lower in the sky now — a sign that fall would soon be here.

"Caw, caw," squawked two crows as they flew by. The birds were real pests. If we didn't keep them away from the farmyard they would eat the grain that I fed the chickens, and they

29

would even dig up the corn seeds that were planted in the garden. They also liked to eat the eggs of the smaller birds.

Soon we were at church and sitting in our usual pew. Just as church was about to begin, I noticed that the Bakers were not seated behind us. They were sitting at the back of the church. The pew in front of us and the pew behind us were empty.

Amy sat beside me, head bent, biting her bottom lip. Father clasped Mother's hand tightly as they exchanged that look again.

The sermon was much too difficult for me to understand and I tried not to squirm in my seat. The sky was starting to fill with dark clouds. They seemed to be huffing and puffing their way across the sky. The weather in Saskatchewan was noted for rapid changes. A strong wind suddenly came up.

BOOM! Thunder roared. Amy and I both jumped. Then we got the giggles.

"If you can't control yourselves, you can leave," the pastor abruptly spoke to us.

We both fell silent.

After church we all quickly boarded the buggy and headed for home. The storm had moved to the east but it looked like another one was moving in.

"We need to get home before the storm hits," Father said.

He urged the horses to run as fast as they could but the storm moved in too fast. We were still a mile from home when the rain came. It was like the heavens had opened its doors and buckets of water were falling upon us. Soon we were all drenched.

"Get under the seat," Father shouted to Amy and I. Mother sat on the floor of the buggy.

"Whoa," Father kept saying to the horses. He was having trouble controlling them.

The horses had a mind of their own. They took off and bounced and banged us around until we were very close to home. A crack of thunder spooked them and there was no holding them back. The buggy over turned and broke loose from the horses. We were thrown to the ground.

"Are you all right?" Father asked as he came to each of us.

"Yes," Mother answered.

"Yes," I replied.

Amy was slow to respond but a yes came from her too.

We had a short walk to the house but the wind and rain made it very difficult. We all held hands to stay together. My pink checkered dress with its heavily gathered ankle length skirt felt like I was dragging a ton of weight.

At home Father found the horses at the barn. Mother, Amy and I went as far as the veranda where we were sheltered from the wind and the rain. The water spilled on the floor in big puddles.

"Quickly get out of your outer clothes and leave them here," Mother said. She did the same and then she brought us all towels.

"Now go to your rooms and get into some dry clothes.

Bring your wet clothes to the kitchen."

"I'm cold," I said as I started to shiver.

"Hurry and change," Mother urged.

When we came back to the kitchen, Mother had a fire going in the wood stove and we huddled around it to keep warm. We hung our clothes on the clothes horse to dry. It had wooden dowels formed into a tent like structure. Mother brought a blanket for Amy and a sweater for me.

Father changed into dry clothes in the porch and soon joined us at the stove.

"This calls for a nice hot cup of cocoa," Mother said and she quickly put milk into a pot and heated it on the stove.

Soon we were all sipping cocoa and reviewing the events of the day. The rain had put a chill in the air but it smelled clean and fresh. It was a welcome relief from the dust that often blew through the air.

"Why doesn't anyone want to sit by us in church?" I asked.

Father replied, "Sometimes people just do not understand that God loves us all for what we are. We try to live a good Christian life but others don't always see life like we do."

"We've chosen to befriend a person in need and I'm sure that God would want us to continue doing so," Mother continued as she smiled at Amy.

"Sometimes our faith is challenged. We must do what we think is right even though others see it in another way."

I wasn't sure that I knew what they meant but I chose not

32

to question it anymore.

"We must forgive, forget and move on," Mother added.

That part of the conversation was over.

"Thank you Mr. and Mrs. Stover."

"Have you ever been in a buggy with run away horses?" Father asked Amy.

"No," Amy replied. "It was very scary."

It had scared me too. This was the third time I was in a run away and each time it was a terrifying event.

Mother rose and said she would start dinner. Amy went to help her. I went to the window to see what was happening. The clouds were busy pouring rain on us so they were hidden. I watched the rain for a while when a thought came to me.

I found the Eaton's catalogue and started turning the pages until I found the babies. I had talked to my parents about getting me a baby sister and they would always reply, "If God wants you to have one, you will get one."

I had prayed for a sister many times but my prayers did not get answered. Maybe I needed to do something about it. I remembered our pastor saying in one of his sermons that the Lord helps those who help themselves. Maybe I needed to help myself get the sister I wanted.

There she is. She would make a nice sister.

I looked at the baby in the catalogue. I was sure she would be just the right one. The dress was all frilly and soft looking. It said that the dress came in pink, white or blue. Pink was

33

my favourite color.

"Amy, would you help me look after a baby sister if we got one?"

"Yes," Amy replied. "I like babies."

"Good."

I picked up a pencil and started to write.

AUGUST 25, 1920

Dear T. Eaton & Company

I want you to send me a baby sister. I am so lonesome and I need someone to play with. Amy lives with us and she will help me take care of her. I would call her Annie. Could you send my sister in a pink dress?

Please send the baby to the post office at Pearl, Saskatchewan.

I will really take good care of her.

Yours truly,

Ellen Stover

I put the letter in the envelope that was in the catalogue. I knew that it had to have a stamp so I asked my mother to put a stamp on it and mail it for me. She said she would.

"How many days before my order comes?" I asked.

"What did you order?" Mother asked.

"A baby sister."

"That's nice," Mother smiled as she replied. "Well, sometimes they get so many orders that they may put your order on hold. It also takes about three days for the letter to get to Winnipeg. By the way, what can you tell me about Winnipeg?"

"It's the capital city of Manitoba. The Red River runs through it and that's where the Eaton company is."

"Very good. now it's time to get washed up for dinner."

I took a dipper full of water from the pail in the porch and emptied it in the washbasin. I then went to the stove for a dipper full of hot water. We had a reservoir at one end of the stove that was filled with water and when the stove was in use it kept the water hot. The cook stove would go out after dinner but the water stayed warm for a long time.

We all gathered at the table and Father said grace. Mother had served a nice dinner of pork chops, mashed potatoes, gravy, beans and vegetable marrow. For dessert she served raspberries and her special crumb cake. It was made with sour cream with cinnamon and a nice crumb topping.

"Amy, you are looking rather pale," Mother said. "Maybe you should lie down after you are finished eating. Ellen can give me a hand with the dishes."

"Thank you, Mrs. Stover. I am very tired."

Mother put hot water from the stove's reservoir into the dish basin and carried it over to the cupboard. She added cold water from a pail, as the water was very hot. When we were done cleaning, I was free to do what I wanted.

"Father, would you like to play a game of checkers?"

"Sure, but you better be prepared to lose."

I knew that Father was a very good checker player. Mother told me that Father was considered one of the best checker players in the area. I think he let me win sometimes. Father had made the checker board and all the moving pieces out of wood. Mother had used red and black paint to complete the set.

"Where did you learn to play checkers?" I asked my father.

"My father taught me when I was your age. He was a very good player and he beat me all the time. He showed me no mercy."

"I don't believe you.

"Well, it's true."

Father won the game just as the sun came out. It was the perfect time to be outdoors. There were puddles to splash in and mud to squeeze between my toes. I was out the door and running for the nearest puddle when Spot came running and jumped all over me. Spot was an old farm dog that we had to help herd the cattle. I was covered with muddy paw marks. We ran around the yard through the puddles and the grass.

The cows were coming toward the barn and Spot went to

follow at their heels making sure all of them came. Mother and Father came out to milk the three cows that we had. Sometimes I milked one.

"Ellen, what have you done? Just look at you. Go in the house and change your clothes before you catch your death of cold," Mother said.

The sun was slowly sinking in the west and the air was chilly. I started to shiver. I went to the house and took off my dress in the porch and headed to my room to change. When I returned, Amy was rinsing the mud out of my dress.

"Ellen, would you carry this basin outside and empty it?"

I knew Amy was not supposed to lift anything so I emptied the basin for her. I shook out my dress and hung it on the clothes horse by the stove.

"Please set the table for me," Amy said.

Mother had stuffed a vegetable marrow with hamburger and it was in the oven along with some scalloped potatoes. Amy had made coleslaw and was slicing bread.

Mother and Father returned from milking. Father had fed the milk to the pigs as we could not use it all. The morning's milk had been put in milk bottles and lowered in a bucket in the well. The air was cool down there.

Mother helped Amy serve supper and then we were free to do what we wanted. Amy excused herself and went to her room. Mother and Father left to go for a walk. They often did this to check on the garden, the fields or the animals to see if everything was in good shape. Plants and animals had to be watched carefully for any sign of disease. It was very important that it was spotted before it spread to other plants or animals. That was all part of being a good farmer.

The air was chilly tonight so I chose to stay indoors. Clouds were moving in again and it looked like more rain. That would be a problem as harvest time required dry conditions.

I sat at the kitchen table with the Eaton's catalogue. I turned the pages and looked for my sister. I would have so much fun with her. We would play together after school and on Saturday and Sunday.

But what would she do while I was in school? I would have to talk to Amy about looking after her. I wonder what Amy will do as she had finished grade eight and our school did not teach any higher grades. Who will care for her?

Mother and Father came in the house.

"Who will look after Amy?" I asked.

"Amy is welcome to stay with us and help out on the farm," Mother replied.

I sighed with relief. Amy would look after my sister when I was in school.

Mother made us some hot cocoa. We always had lots of milk for things like that. Tonight she served toast as well. I looked out the window for a nice cloud. I heard thunder.

I changed into my nightgown and crawled into bed. The thunder was louder now and lightning was flashing across the sky. And then the rain came. Plop! Plop! The roof was leaking again. Water was dripping near the foot of my bed. I called for

Mother to come and see. She brought a pail to catch the water.

I tried so hard to fall asleep but the constant plop of the water in the pail was very annoying. I tried counting sheep. It did not work.

It seemed ever so long before the rain quieted. I went to the window and saw stars in the sky. The dark clouds had moved away leaving one small one behind for me.

Be strong, Ellen! Be strong!

Chapter 4

"I LEFT THE thunder mug on the veranda," Father said as he came into the kitchen.

"What's a thunder mug?" Amy asked.

"A thunder mug is a chamber pail," Mother replied.

A chamber pail was an enamel container with a lid that was used at night as a toilet. It was my job to wash and disinfect it and return it to the upper level of the house where the bedrooms were located.

It was a sunny day in early September and I spotted a horse and buggy coming up the lane.

"Mother, there's someone coming."

We seldom had visitors anymore so this was exciting. Mother went outside to greet the visitor. It was Mrs. Hogan, a lady that lived in town.

"Welcome Elsie, How are you?"

"I'm fine."

"Come in and have coffee with us."

"Thanks, I will."

Father said he was going to the barn. He greeted Mrs. Hogan and then proceeded to take her horse over to the barn where he gave it some water and tied it to a post.

We all went into the kitchen with Mother.

"Have a chair Elsie. What brings you here?"

"It is such a lovely day that I thought it would be nice to have a ride in the country and visit with you. I haven't seen you for quite some time. How have you been feeling?"

"The pain is getting a little worse," my mother replied.

That was a strange answer. I never knew Mother to have any pain. She was always busy doing things. I would have liked to ask what she was talking about but I could only speak if I was spoken to and that was the way it was. Children were supposed to be seen and not heard.

"How is Jack?" Mother asked. Jack was Mrs. Hogan's husband.

"He's just fine. Very busy at the lumberyard, now that the harvest is over. Everyone seems to be fixing or building. But that's good."

Mother had put a pot of coffee on and was cutting some coffee cake.

"Go call your father for coffee Ellen."

I went outside looking for Father but couldn't see him so I headed in the general direction of the barn.

41

"Father," I called.

He came to the barn door and said, "What is it?"

"Come for coffee."

"Be right there."

As I was nearing the house, I heard my mother say, "It won't be much longer before I will be bedridden. The doctor has given me two months to a year."

What was she talking about?

I opened the door and went into the kitchen.

"Come, sit here Ellen."

They were all seated at the table.

"Did you find your father?"

"Yes, he will be here right away."

Father came in the porch, washed his hands and joined us at the table.

"How are you Elsie?" Father asked.

"Just fine," she replied. "I bet you're very happy to have the harvest done."

"Oh yes. It was a good one too."

I was so hungry that I was stuffing coffee cake in my mouth.

Mother said, "Slow down Ellen! Chew your food."

I immediately slowed down but not much.

"May I be excused?" I asked. I did not want to be a part of this conversation. I had things to do like looking for bees, butterflies and other flying creatures.

"Yes, you may," my mother responded.

I was off to chase the critters. The hummingbirds had gone to their winter home and I missed them. They would fly and fight with one another over the flowers. They were so colourful in their reds and greens.

We had two or three light frosts and most of the flowers were gone now so the birds would not have any food.

Father left the house and went back to the barn. He was probably not interested in the chatter of the ladies.

I could not find any critters so I knew that fall was here and that winter would not be far behind.

Mrs. Hogan and Mother came to the door.

"Would you ask your father to bring Mrs. Hogan's horse and buggy to the house, Ellen?"

"Yes, Mother."

I skipped my way to the barn to deliver the message.

Soon Mrs. Hogan was on her way.

Father turned to Mother and said, "I buried the money under the cross of the boy."

Mother replied, "Good idea."

I did not know what they were talking about. The clouds would understand; they absorbed all my thoughts and deeds and took them to the heavens.

The days passed slowly. I was looking forward to going back to school.

On the fifteenth of September Mother called me to the kitchen. "There is a letter here for you from the T. Eaton Company."

My heart started to pound. I tried to open it but my fingers just couldn't seem to manage it. Mother helped me.

Where was my baby sister? Was the company telling me where to pick her up?

Many thoughts were racing through my mind.

SEPTEMBER 8, 1920

Dear Miss Stover:

Thank you for your letter of August 25, 1920. We will be glad to send you a sister.

We regret to inform you that we have had so many requests for baby girls this year that we have to put your request on back order. Your shipment should arrive in late December. We hope that this does not cause you any inconvenience.

Sincerely,

D. Black,
Customer Service,
T. Eaton & Company,
Winnipeg, Manitoba

"But that is such a long time," I said sadly.
Mother hugged me and said, "The time will go by quickly.

You will soon be busy with your studies at school."

I choked and a tear ran down my cheek. I needed to find a cloud.

"Why don't you see how Amy is doing?"

Amy was busy with some needlework. "What are you making?"

"A blanket for your sister."

"It's so pretty Amy. I like the patchwork quilt because it has lots of pink."

That cheered me up and I went back outdoors to check for critters.

The time did pass and school opened on September twentieth. I looked forward to learning new things but I wondered how I would be treated. I was an outcast in the church and the town children avoided me.

I loved to learn about far away places. We were to have a new teacher. Maybe she came from Ontario or Alberta.

Most farm people attended small country schools but we lived less that two miles from town so I joined the town children. On the first day of school I arrived fifteen minutes early and several students were already there playing ball and skipping rope. I watched from a distance. Other students arrived and they were asked to join in the game.

A lady was holding the hand of a new student. I did not know who they were. They went into the school and soon the lady left. The girl remained in the one room school.

The bell rang. Miss Walkerton, our new teacher, intro-

45

duced herself and asked us each to rise and tell our name and grade. The new girl was Betsy Connor and she was in grade three. She was very pretty with haunting dark eyes and dark hair. Her dress was very worn and her shoes were cut open at the toes to accommodate feet that were too big for them.

Miss Walkerton welcomed us all and hoped that we would all have a good year. She then started handing out books, scribblers and pencils. At recess we were all asked to go outdoors to get some sunshine and fresh air.

No one minded this time of the year as fall was cool but if you played hard you would stay warm. I walked around the schoolyard and asked if I could join the ball game. One said that I should go out in left field. That was the place that they put the poorest player. When our team left the field, I never got asked to bat.

Betsy stood alone by the school. She was the first to enter the classroom when the bell rang calling us to class.

In the classroom one grade eight girl whispered to me, "Is the prostitute still living at your house?"

I had since learned what the word meant and I was very upset. I replied, "Amy is not a prostitute. She is a very nice girl."

Several children snickered around me.

I knew from that moment that they would make my life very difficult. I would be spending much time by myself.

After school Miss Walkerton called me aside, "Ellen," she said. "I think Betsy could use a friend. I bet she would love to have you for a friend."

46

I wasn't sure about that but I replied, "Yes, Miss Walkerton, I'll try tomorrow."

With that I was on my way home. I walked slowly so that I would not have to be near the students that were headed in the same direction. I had had enough snickering and finger pointing for one day.

I looked upward. The clouds were floating ever so slow. My steps slowed to their pace.

Help me get through the day.

I was very sad watching the children laugh and skip on their way home. I should be doing the same.

Go home Ellen. Mother and Amy will be glad to see you. Go home Ellen. Go home.

Chapter 5

I TOLD MOTHER and Amy about the new girl at school and that Miss Walkerton thought that I might like to be her new friend. Mother thought that was a great idea. Amy seldom offered any comments or advice but today she did, "That's a very good idea. It must be very hard to start school in a new town."

"Betsy seems to be very poor as her dress was pretty faded and she had holes in her shoes so that her toes had room."

"That's too bad," Mother replied. "Never judge a book by its cover."

I knew that she meant that I should not judge Betsy by her clothing. She could be a very fine person. I left for school excited about meeting Betsy. I wondered what I should say to her.

Hello Betsy, my name is Ellen. Would you like to seesaw with me? No, that wouldn't work. Lots of girls hated the seesaw as the boys liked to dump them.

Maybe I should just ask her to walk home with me after school.

It turned out that I did not have to talk to her first. I walked directly by her house on the way to school. Her mother came out with Betsy to say good-bye to her.

When she saw me, Betsy's mother said, "Good morning young lady. How are you?"

"Fine," I replied.

"Could Betsy walk to school with you this morning?"

"Sure."

"Run along now, Betsy. See you at dinner time."

Betsy joined me. She looked at the ground as we walked along. That was what Amy did. Mother said she needed to build up her self-confidence, whatever that meant.

"Do you like school?" I asked.

"I do but I have no friends here and it's scary having no friends."

"Don't be scared. I will be your friend if you like."

"Oh, yes," she said.

With that we both skipped along and soon we were at the school.

Miss Walkerton was there to greet us. "Are you two getting to know one another?" she asked.

"Yes," we both said at the same time.

"I'm glad," Miss Walkerton replied.

She rang the bell calling the students to class.

The first class of the day was Reading. Miss Walkerton taught all eight grades. There were only two or three students per class but there were a lot of grades to teach. She was very patient and tried her best to give equal time to all grades.

I looked forward to recess today.

"Do you want to play on the swings?" I asked Betsy.

"Sure."

We headed in the direction of the swings. When we passed two girls they snickered and turned away. I was used to this treatment at church. It upset Betsy. It still upset me but I knew I had to hide my feelings so that Betsy would have someone to stand by her. Amy and I often looked out for one another.

"Why are they laughing at us?" she asked.

"Sometimes girls just don't know what they are saying. We just have to forgive, forget and move on. Do you want me to push you on the swing?" I asked.

"Yes."

Recess passed quickly and so did my Arithmetic class. At noon I ate my lunch alone out on the swing. Betsy went home for hers.

After school we left together. A couple of boys shoved us and called us stupid and then ran away.

"We must forgive, forget and move on," I said when I saw a tear roll from Betsy's eye.

"It's just so hard. It makes me feel so sad."

"It's all right to feel sad. But I'm your friend now. I understand."

50

Betsy smiled and said, "Friends forever?"

"Friends forever," I replied.

"Race you home," she said.

We were off. I was able to beat her by just a little. We were both laughing as I left her at her gate. I had a great walk home. I could hardly wait to tell Mother and Amy about my day. The clouds were ever so soft today. One even had a great big smile for me.

As I neared the house, Amy came out to greet me.

"Your mother isn't feeling well," she said.

"What's wrong?"

"She has a flu, I think and she doesn't want any of us to get it. Here, let me take your books inside and I'll bring you out a nice snack and we will have it on the veranda."

"All right," I said as I handed her my books.

Mother seemed to be getting sick quite often with a flu bug. She somehow was not her usual happy self.

Amy returned with peanut butter cookies and milk. Were they ever good.

"I made these cookies especially for you," she said. "You have been such a big help for me."

Amy was referring to her school lessons that I took to Miss Walkerton for her. Mother had helped her get correspondence courses to complete her high school. She would finish them in the spring if she worked hard.

Mother had talked to Miss Walkerton about helping Amy. She said she would be glad to but she just couldn't come to

51

our house. Amy had to send her questions to school with me. Her notes were tucked inside mine.

"Oh Amy, I have a new friend. Remember the new girl I talked about yesterday? Her name is Betsy and she is really nice. She is so unhappy though."

"Oh, I'm sure you will fix that for her. Being her friend will help."

"They live in that old house on the edge of town where nobody has lived for a long time."

"I know which one you mean, the old Pepperton house."

"Yes, that's the one."

"Betsy is in grade three and Miss Walkerton is teaching her some grade four work. She seems to be awfully smart."

"Good for her," Amy replied. "Now it's time for me to get back to my studies. Do you have any homework?"

"A little," I replied.

"Come along then. Change your clothes and join me at the kitchen table. Let's try to be quiet so that we don't wake your mother."

We quietly went into the house. I quickly changed my clothes and joined Amy at the table. I would much rather watch the clouds right now. They were so soft and fluffy today.

"Hello Ellen," Amy whispered. "You're day dreaming again."

I picked up my reader and opened it. The clouds would have to play without me.

Father came in and went to see Mother.

"Ellen, I need you to milk a cow for me," he said when he returned.

I went to the barn and found my stool and milk pail and headed to Daisy's stall. I sat down on my stool and prepared to milk. I petted Daisy on her stomach. She gave me a friendly moo. Then she swished her tail and hit me on the head. It was a gentle swish so I knew she was glad to see me. She was drying up so I got less than half a pail of milk.

Father and I took the milk to the house where Amy bottled it. Father then took all but one bottle to the well where he put them to stay cool.

Amy had supper ready for us. She had taken Mother a bowl of soup earlier; she was just too weak to join us at the table.

Father said grace and we feasted on boiled potatoes, cooked cabbage, hamburger, fried onions and sliced tomatoes. Amy served some canned strawberries that Mother had picked and processed in the spring. She also served some more peanut butter cookies. She was so good to me.

After supper I helped Amy clean up the kitchen. I found the Eaton's catalogue and gazed fondly at my sister. It was going to take forever before she came.

Amy sat at the kitchen writing in her diary.

"Why can't you go home Amy?" I asked.

She replied, "My father told me that I had sinned and that I would burn in hell. He beat me and beat me and then threw me out the door and told me never to come back."

"That must have been awful." I remembered clearly how

she had looked that day.

"Didn't your mother help you?" I asked.

"No, she just stood in the doorway with tears running down her face."

"Why did you come to our house?"

"I just walked and walked for what seemed like hours. I spotted your house and you know the rest."

"Do you like living with us?"

"Yes, but I am very lonely. I should have friends my own age and I should be thinking about marriage and children. I don't think that will ever happen."

"What will you do?"

"I will study hard and try to become a teacher so I can work with children. I shouldn't be so lonely then. You are so lucky Ellen to have such good parents."

"I guess so."

"Your mother told me that I did not do anything wrong or bad and that God will take care of me. She said my name meant beloved or dearly loved and that God loves me just as I am."

"I know He does because He takes care of all of us. Can I have another peanut butter cookie?"

"Oh Ellen, you sure can. Just one with a glass of milk and then it is off to bed so you are rested for school."

"Will you come back to Pearl and be my teacher?"

"I don't think so."

"But I will miss you."

"And I will miss you and your mother and father. Now I

54

have to study."

I went upstairs to say good night to Mother. I thought she was asleep but she called out to me, "Come in Ellen but don't come too close. I don't want you to get sick. How was school today?"

"It was good. Betsy is my new friend and we promised to be friends forever."

"That's nice. Everyone needs a friend. You will make one or two great friends in a lifetime. If you make more you will be a very fortunate person."

"I think Amy needs a friend."

"I know she does and I hope that someday she will find one. Now say your prayers and go to bed. Good night Ellen. I love you."

"Good night Mother. I love you."

I went to my room and headed straight for the window.

Clouds were softly floating in the sky.

I lay awake in bed for a long time. There were so many questions that needed to be answered.

Why won't anyone talk to us at church? What did we do? What did Amy do that her father said that she would rot in hell? Why wouldn't her mother help her? Why was my Mother so sick again?

I quietly crept to the window one more time. The moon was out lighting up the sky for one lonesome cloud. I'm sure it was glad to see me.

Amy will have a friend some day. Be good to your friend Betsy. Good friends are hard to find.

55

Chapter 6

WE SANG *O Canada* every morning before we started our classes at school but we practiced the song a few more times so that the new students knew all the words.

This morning we sang:

O Canada! Our home and native land!
True patriot love in all thy sons command.
With glowing hearts we see thee rise,
The true North strong and free,
And stand on guard, O Canada;
We stand on guard for thee.
O Canada! Glorious and free!
We stand on guard; we stand on guard for thee.
O Canada! We stand on guard for thee.

Miss Walkerton then said, "The music for *O Canada* was written by Calixa Lavallee of Vercheres, Quebec. The English words were written by Robert Stanley Weir. It was first sung publicly in 1880. This information in written on the chalk board; please copy it into your Literature notebook."

School had been going for several weeks now and it was time to prepare for tests and Open House. We would write our tests, Miss Walkerton would grade them and then we would set a day for parents to come and visit the school. Friday, November the twenty-sixth was the day. At one o'clock in the afternoon the program for Open House would begin.

When our tests were completed, we spent a lot of time preparing the program for Open House. The singing, reciting and acting were all a big part in our public schooling. We did a lot of memory work.

When Friday arrived Betsy said, "I'm real scared about my speech." She had to give the welcome speech.

I replied. "You will do fine. Just look at me and pretend that you are just talking to me about the program."

The program was opened with the singing of *O Canada* followed by the parish priest leading us in *The Lord's Prayer.* Then it was Betsy's turn.

She looked at me and began, "Miss Walkerton, parents, friends and students, welcome to Open House. We have worked hard to prepare for this day and Miss Walkerton has been a great leader. Following the program there will be coffee, juice and cookies for everyone. We hope you enjoy the program."

Betsy looked at me the whole time that she spoke and I smiled and shook my head up and down for her. She received a round of applause when she was finished. She proudly took her seat.

The program went well. There were recitations, songs and a skit put on by the older students. The songs we sang were *Clementine, Camptown Races* and *I've Been Working on the Railroad*. Just before the closing of the program with the singing of *God Save the King,* Mr. Eastman thanked Miss Walkerton and the students for a wonderful afternoon.

Miss Walkerton asked for everyone's attention as she said, "Please look at the art, printing and writing that is displayed on the walls. You can pick up your child's report card and talk to me about any concerns that you may have. In the meantime enjoy some cookies."

The school families took turns in providing lunches for our school activities.

My parents were pleased with my progress and complimented Miss Walkerton on the job she was doing. Amy had come to the school and she was waiting at the back of the room for us.

"Come with us for cookies and a drink, Amy," Mother said.

She reluctantly followed us to the table where two older students were serving. The girls served my parents and I but refused to offer Amy anything. She was about to turn around to leave when my father grabbed her arm.

He said in a very powerful voice, "Amy will have two cookies and a glass of juice."

58

The girls quickly handed her a glass of juice and a plate with two cookies.

"Thank you," Amy said meekly. She was biting her bottom lip again trying not to cry.

We all found chairs and sat down to have our lunch. Everyone avoided us except Betsy and her mother. Betsy's father did not come. Her mother said that he was indisposed. I wasn't sure what that meant.

Betsy had such a great report card that Miss Walkerton said she was going to promote her to grade four in the new year. She could then join me and two other students; she would not have to be the only one in her class.

"But I'm the smartest in my class now," she said with a grin.

We had a good chuckle at her comment.

"Then, on the other hand, I'm also the dumbest in my class," she continued. "Whom shall I be today?"

"Be smart," I answered. "That's the best way to be."

It was time to gather up our things and head for home. The days were very short now and no one wanted to travel after dark if it was not necessary.

When we were in the buggy on our way home, Amy was very quiet. I was busy looking for a special cloud. Today it was very dark and the clouds seemed sad.

"It will probably snow tonight," Father said.

We had some snow earlier in the year but very little remained. Pretty soon we would have lots of snow and we would then be traveling in a van that the horses would pull. It was equipped with a small wood stove and wooden benches. It was like a mini house on runners.

It was rather chilly riding in an open buggy so I looked forward to some snow because we needed the snow to cover the ground before the runners would work.

Send some snow please, oh great and mighty cloud.

My wish was granted that night. We woke up to a foot of snow. Father harnessed up the horses and hooked them up to the van to go to town. He always made a trail for me with the runners of the van so that I could walk in the grooves when I went to school. Father had a fire in the stove and it was nice and cozy.

We started doing our weekly shopping in the morning or afternoon on Saturdays now. Our social life on Saturday night had become nothing so we felt it was better to get things done during daylight hours.

Sunday church service became a new ritual for us. We arrived just in time for the service to start and we left immediately after it was over.

On Monday morning Father hooked up the van and took me to school. He had a nice fire going.

"I'll pick you up after school," he said. "Pay attention to the teacher."

"Yes, Father. Bye."

"Bye Ellen."

I took my books into the school and headed out to play in the snow. That was not such a good idea. The older boys were busy making snowballs and throwing them. One hit me in the face and it stung so hard that it brought tears to my eyes.

Betsy arrived and was hit also. Soon they decided that Betsy and I were their targets and they kept hitting us with snowballs. We were forced to go inside.

"Good morning girls," Miss Walkerton said. "Would you two like to memorize and recite the poem *'Twas the Night Before Christmas* for the Christmas concert?"

We both agreed that we could do it. The concert would be on Friday the seventeenth of December; that was less than three weeks away.

"We will have to do some practicing together," I said.

"I'm not allowed to bring anyone home with me," Betsy replied.

"Maybe you can come home with me after school and spend the night with us?"

"I will have to ask my mother."

"We can always practice at noon hour if you come back early," I said.

"Sure or maybe we could stay after school, Miss Walkerton?"

"I'm sure that can be arranged," Miss Walkerton replied.

Miss Walkerton rang the bell and another school day began.

When Father picked me up after school, I asked, "Can Betsy come to our house to practice a poem for the Christmas concert?"

"We'll have to talk this over with your mother. She hasn't been feeling that good and she needs her rest," Father replied.

Mother was resting when we got home so I quickly changed my clothes and met Amy at the kitchen table. She was busy writing in her diary.

At suppertime I asked Mother if Betsy could visit one night next week. Mother looked very tired and her voice was weak when she replied, "I'm sure we can work something out."

"Thank you Mother."

"Amy would you write me a note to Mrs. Connor asking her if Betsy could spend the night?" Mother asked.

"Sure, Mrs. Stover," the reply came.

"Can we do it next Monday?" I asked.

"That's fine with me," Mother replied. "How about you Henry? Are you available to drive the girls to and from school?"

"Yes, I'm sure I can."

I did walk to school on very cold days, but Betsy was not used to such a long walk on a cold day so we would use the van.

"You know it will soon be December and it won't be long before I get my baby sister. I hope that Eaton's hasn't forgotten her."

"I don't think so," Father replied. "They are very reliable when it comes to filling orders."

"We will have to find your baby clothes and get them ready for her," Mother added.

"What name do you want for your sister?"

"Annie," I replied instantly.

"That's a fine name," Father replied. "What do you think about having an Annie for a daughter?"

"I think it's a great name. What about you Amy? Do you like the name Annie? The name means that God has been gracious."

"It's a nice name," Amy replied.

"I think I will start knitting her a blanket," I said. "Can I have some yarn?"

"May I have some yarn?" Mother corrected me.

"May I have some yarn please?"

"Yes, you may."

I could pass the time knitting now. The days were too cold for playing outside. I would knit the blanket in small squares and then I would sew the squares together. Mother had taught me to knit when I was six years old and my stitches were very even. The evening passed quickly.

At bedtime I was very tired and dropped off to sleep right away. I did not have time to talk to the clouds.

In the morning I took the note that Amy had written, bundled myself up with a scarf over my face and headed off to school. It was cold but we were used to living in this type of climate.

Betsy met me at her gate with a big smile and I said, "Good morning Betsy. I have a note for your mother asking if you can come to our house next Monday."

"Good, I'll take it to her now."

Betsy took the note to the house but we did not have time to wait for an answer. She went home at noon hour and we would learn the answer then.

Later that morning Father came to the school with a load of wood for the stove. Parents of school children often donated stuff to the school. He was unloading the wood at recess time and Miss Walkerton asked the older boys to go outside and help him. They did go and give him a hand.

The Christmas program was prepared for us and we all had something to do. Mother usually played the piano for the concert but this year she was not strong enough. One of the grade eight girls had the honour this year. Mother had taught me to play at age six but I did not feel that I was good enough to play at the concert.

At noon I ate my lunch alone in my desk waiting for Betsy to return. When she did, she looked sad.

"Mother said I couldn't impose on your family," she said.

I was disappointed and so I said, "Can you come back early at noon to practice?"

"Yes," she replied. "My mother thought that would be a better idea."

That was all right with me as my noon hours were long and lonely. I often spent my time reading or just doing any homework that was assigned that morning. Miss Walkerton was always there at noon hour so that the students did have some time to do their assignments. Often the older children had to spend all their time helping out with the chores at home.

At the end of the school day the sky was clear and the temperature was dropping so I would have to walk as fast as I could. There was no time for daydreaming.

Where are you today? Have you gone to a warmer place?

Chapter 7

"MOTHER, BUBBLIN' Bob is coming up the lane," I said.

"Ellen, that's Mr. Jones to you," Mother replied.

"Yes, Mother. Sorry."

"Go get your father."

Bob Jones was a neighbor who lived a mile from us. He seemed to forget how to get home sometimes. He was nicknamed *Bubblin' Bob* because he was always laughing and singing. Today, he was singing as I headed to the barn to find Father.

"*Oh, the moon shines bright on Bessie Cartwright, She couldn't fart right, Her butt was air tight,*" sang Bubblin' Bob.

He was singing the words to the tune of *Red Wing*.

Father came out of the barn and said to me, "Go in the house Ellen."

"Hey, little girl," called Bubblin' Bob. "Come, pull my finger."

"No thanks," I replied. I wasn't getting caught on that again. I pulled his finger once and he farted.

"Who's Bessie Cartwright?" I asked Mother as I entered the kitchen.

"Is Mr. Jones singing about her again?" she asked.

"Yes."

"Well, you best forget what you heard," Mother responded. "He shouldn't be singing songs like that in front of children."

Father brought Mr. Jones into the house and asked Mother, "Can you find something for Bob to eat? I'm going to saddle up Dong."

Dong was one of the horses that pulled our buggy. The other horse was Ding. We did not ride horseback very often and when we did, the same horses that worked as a team to pull the buggy were used.

Mother served Mr. Jones some stew, bread and coffee.

"Thank you Mary," he said.

Father returned and helped Mr. Jones into his buggy. Bubblin' Bob was having trouble walking. He seemed to be stumbling a lot. Father had hitched Dong to the end of the buggy and the horse would follow along as Father took Mr. Jones home.

"*Oh the moon shines bright on Bessie ---,*" Bubblin' Bob's voice faded as they moved down the lane.

Father would take him home and then come back on horseback.

"You can come out now Amy," Mother said.

Amy came out to the kitchen and started getting supper ready. Supper would be late tonight as it would be a while before Father returned.

Mother was embroidering a tablecloth. "Have you ever had the urge to do something wild and crazy?" she asked me.

"Like what?"

"Like painting the town red."

"What does painting the town red mean?"

"It means going out and having a good time."

"Sure," I replied. "That would be fun."

"Well, everyone should do something wild and crazy at least once in her lifetime."

I picked up my knitting and I thought about what Mother had said. We both worked on our projects until Father came in for supper.

The next day was very cold. It was the last day of school before the Christmas holidays started. I bundled up, wrapping a long scarf around my face.

"I'll take you to school Ellen," Father said. "It's very cold and I need some nails."

"Thanks," I said. I welcomed the warm and cozy van ride.

At school, the day was filled with last minute preparations for the concert. Betsy and I had practiced at noon hours and after school so we both knew our lines well.

We were let out of school at noon as we would have to return again for the seven o'clock concert that evening.

At home that afternoon Amy helped me wash my hair and then she braided my long brunette hair into a single braid that hung down my back. I liked that better than the two pig tails that were often tied at the back of my head. The clothes that I would wear were laying on my bed. I had a new pink dress that was frilly and had lots of lace.

That evening we all went to the concert. Mother felt strong and Amy seemed happy to go. Christmas cheer seemed to be everywhere.

The schoolhouse was packed with people for the event.

Betsy's father did not come. I know she felt bad that he did not take part in her life. Betsy told me that he drank a lot of beer and hung around the house while her mother worked hard cleaning for other people.

Miss Walkerton welcomed everyone to the concert and asked us all to rise for the singing of O Canada.

The first items on the program were limericks that the grade one and two students had made up. Helen, a grade one student, came to the front of the room and did her recitation.

> *There came a man from Pearl,*
> *Who looked much like a girl.*
> *He grew long hair*
> *And said, "I care*
> *That my hair is all in curl."*

Helen returned to her seat as everyone clapped.

The next performer was a grade two student by the name of Billy Jones, a nephew of Bubblin' Bob. He began,

Santa comes to see us here
On Christmas Eve each year
He brings us toys
And many joys
And lots and lots of beer.

Everyone was silent for a moment. Miss Walkerton had a strange look on her face. Then the audience burst out laughing and gave Billy a big applause. After all, he was Bubblin' Bob's relative.

The older boys had coached Billy to use beer in his last line instead of cheer. We were not sure if Billy did this on purpose or if he just got excited and said the wrong line.

The students then sang *We Wish You a Merry Christmas* and *Jingle Bells*. Then another limerick was recited by a grade two student.

There was a man who had a dog,
A cat, a mouse, a hog.
The man did play
With them all day
And lost them in the fog.

It was now time for Betsy and I to recite our poem by Clement Clarke Moore.

"*Twas the night before Christmas and all through the house,*" we began in unison. Our recitation went well and now we could relax.

All the students sang *O Little Town of Bethlehem* and *Joy to the World.*

The older students put on a short play. Following this the pianist started to play *Up on the Housetop* and bells started to jingle and we knew Santa Claus was just outside the door. And there he was dressed in his bright red suit trimmed with white fur. He had a long beard and a big smile as he came in ringing a bell and saying, "Ho, ho, ho!"

His voice sounded like Bubblin' Bob, "Were you all good this year?"

"Yes, yes, yes," came the replies.

"Then I have a gift for you."

We all waited with great excitement. *Who would Santa talk to?* He reached into his bag and called out Betsy's name. She was beaming as she collected her present and said thanks to him.

Santa had a present for each of the students and one for Miss Walkerton. Mr. and Mrs. Eastman handed out brown paper bags to all the students and the children that were too young to go to school. The bags were filled with nuts and candies.

Everybody was always so happy at the concert.

Miss Walkerton thanked everyone for coming. Then she asked us all to stand and sing our respect to King George V, the King of England. Canada was a colony and we were under English rule.

God save our gracious King,
Long live our noble King;
God save the King!
Send him victorious,
Happy and glorious,
Long to reign over us,
God save the King!

The concert was over and school was officially closed until February. January was such a cold month that the wood stove could not keep the schoolroom warm enough. The cold winds would blow hard and come in around the windows and the doors and ice would build up on the windows.

We waited inside until Father brought the van to the door. I said good-bye to Betsy and wished her a Merry Christmas. She returned the wish and we left for home.

The sky was filled with dark clouds. They did not look very friendly tonight.

"We're in for a good blizzard," Father said as he urged the horses to go faster.

He was right. Just as we pulled into the yard snow started to fall. We could hardly see our way to the house. The clouds were dumping flakes and flakes and flakes of snow on us. Father found the wire that he had strung from the house to the barn for times like this. He walked the horses to the barn holding onto the line so that he would not loose his way in the storm.

The rest of us went into the house and shook the snow off our clothing in the porch. There were still coals in the wood stove and Mother added some kindling and wood, and soon heat was filling the kitchen.

We all had some hot cocoa and Christmas cake that was full of fruit and nuts. We talked about the concert. Everyone had to admit that Billy stole the evening.

I was very tired so I said good night to everyone and headed to my room. I could not see outside as my window pane was all frosted. There would be nothing to see. The sky would be filled with millions of fluffy flakes.

Have fun my special snow clouds. Thank you for waiting until we were safely home before you shed your snow flakes. Merry Christmas one and all and to all a good night.

Chapter 8

I MISSED GOING to school every day. I missed Betsy. Amy was teaching me to embroider but my fingers just didn't want to make nice even stitches. She was working on a patchwork quilt that would take a long, long time to make. It was all hand stitched and made from old clothes that I had outgrown.

Mother spent most of her days in bed now. She hardly spoke. The doctor came to see her every week now and he would spend a few minutes with her and then he would give Amy some medicine to give Mother for the pain.

"What's wrong with Mother?" I asked.

"She is just so very tired," Amy would reply. "She needs lots of rest."

We worked and played quietly around the house. Sometimes we would go in the far corner of the living room and

Amy would read quietly to me. She still spent a lot of time on her schooling and she was doing well. Mother had told me so.

Father and I would go to town and do the shopping now. Amy stayed at home to look after Mother when we went. Mother did not go to church any more. She was just too frail. The pastor came one day and gave her communion but he did not stay for dinner.

One day Amy told me that my mother wanted to see me. I quietly went into her bedroom.

"Amy said you wanted to see me."

"Sit down beside me on the bed," she said. Her voice was quite strong today and she looked much better. "How are you doing?" she asked.

"Fine," I said. "I am still knitting my blanket for my sister and Amy is teaching me to embroider."

"That's good. Are you reading every day?"

"Yes."

"Do you sometimes hear a voice in your head telling you to do something?"

"Yes Mother I think I do sometimes."

"Listen to it carefully. That voice will guide you through good times and troubled times. Promise me you will always listen to that little voice before you make decisions in your life."

"Yes, Mother I promise."

"Thank you Ellen. Do you go outside every day for some fresh air? It's very important that you get some sunshine even though it is cold."

"Yes. Father takes me to the barn with him and I play outside for a while."

"Christmas will soon be here and I'm counting on you to help Amy out. The Hogans will be coming for dinner."

Mother closed her eyes and drifted off to sleep. I quietly got up and left the room. The day was overcast. The sky was just one big dark cloud. We would surely get some snow today.

Amy and I started preparing for Christmas dinner. We dug out a sour head of cabbage from under the sauerkraut that we had made in the fall. Amy mixed up the rice filling with onions, hamburger, salt and pepper. We tore the leaves off the cabbage head and rinsed them in cold water. Then we stuffed the leaves with the rice mixture and carefully rolled them so the filling would not come out. We placed the cabbage rolls in a large roasting pan and took them to the root cellar when we were done.

Mother had helped Amy make Christmas cake back in November. The fruit cake needed to be aged to make it taste good. It was stored in the root cellar in a crock. They had also made Christmas pudding with suet and lots of dried fruits and nuts. The pudding was placed in sealers and cooked in boiling water to seal. We had several jars to eat throughout the winter.

Tomorrow Amy would make a sauce for the Christmas pudding. We had lots of pickles in the root cellar. We had lots of canned corn and peas and carrots. We would cook a big pot of potatoes and mash them on Christmas Day.

I was tired that night when I went to bed. We would have a very busy day tomorrow as we would be making perogies. I said good night to the clouds that were out there somewhere. There was still ice on the window and it would be there most days until spring came in March.

In the morning right after breakfast Amy and I set to work making perogies. She mixed up the dough with left over mashed potatoes, flour, salt, baking powder, melted lard and an egg. She set it near the stove to keep it warm so the dough could rise and soften. Amy had me make the filling for the perogies. I used cottage cheese, mashed potatoes, onions, an egg and salt and pepper. I had to lightly fry the onions first before I added them to the mixture.

Amy rolled out some of the dough and cut it into small squares. We made smaller perogies when we served a big meal. Later we made larger perogies. We would have those for supper. We boiled them in salted water and then we poured melted butter and fried onions over them just before serving.

Amy made a sauce for the plum pudding by boiling brown sugar and water for a long time. The mixture would thicken and become like a syrup. She added vanilla and put the sauce in the root cellar to keep it cool until tomorrow which was Christmas Day.

Father had brought the few tree ornaments down from the attic. Later that evening we would decorate the tree. Amy and I popped some corn so that we could string them together to make a garland to decorate the tree.

I dusted and cleaned the living room and got a spot ready for the Christmas tree. Father and I had gone out into the bushes near the house and cut our own tree. Father had planted evergreen trees many years ago and we now used one every year. The trees were planted in two rows that were twenty feet apart. Father explained to me that we would use every other one in the rows as it would give the other trees room to grow. The trees sheltered us from the strong north winds. Father put the Christmas tree into a stand that he had made from wood. Mother had painted it green. The trunk of the tree was set in a bowl of water.

"How come an evergreen tree doesn't lose its needles in the winter?" I asked.

"It is a coniferous tree which means that it doesn't drop its leaves. The needles of the trees are their leaves," Amy replied.

"Why do all the other trees lose their leaves in the fall?" I asked.

"They are deciduous trees," Amy answered. "That is a normal way for them to grow. They go to sleep for the winter and grow again in the spring."

"The evergreen tree also provides some colour to the farmyard. They got their name because they are ever or always green. The prairie skyline would look quite drab in the winter without their colour," Father added.

Father helped Mother to a chair in the living room so that she could watch us decorate the tree. We strung the popcorn with long pieces of string and then we placed the strings on the tree. We added some paper ornaments, some of which I had made at school.

An angel dressed in white cloth wings and gown was

placed on top of the tree. It was my grandmother's angel. Mother treasured it as that was the only thing she had from her mother. My grandparents had stayed in Europe when my parents came to Canada.

"Are you excited Ellen?" Mother asked.

"Yes. I don't know why Eaton's hasn't sent my baby sister."

"December isn't over yet. I'm sure she will come," Mother said.

Amy served some hot apple cider and some Christmas cake. I kept wondering what would be under the tree for me in the morning.

"Off to bed, Ellen," Father said. "We have a busy day tomorrow."

I said good night and went to bed. Before I drifted off to sleep there were many questions that I needed answered.

When will my baby sister come? When will Mother get well? Is Amy happy with us?

Life seemed to be full of questions that needed answers.

Be still, Ellen. Everything will be fine. Enjoy your Christmas.

I loved Christmas time. Everyone seemed to be happy.

Was that the voice that Mother was talking about? It was in my head. I always thought the clouds were talking to me. The voice came again telling me to sleep well.

I closed my eyes and the next thing I heard was Amy calling me, "Merry Christmas Ellen. It's time to get up. I need your help."

I jumped out of bed and dressed quickly. It was Christmas

Day. The door to the living room was closed and we would not be allowed in until our guests had arrived. We would then exchange and open our gifts.

Amy prepared a turkey and put it in the oven. I scratched some frost off the kitchen window to make a peep hole so that I could see the Hogans come up the lane. It was a sunny day with just a few clouds floating around looking for a friend to play with. I wouldn't have time to watch them today.

The Hogans arrived with gifts for everyone. Father helped Mother to the living room where we gathered around the Christmas tree. Since I was the youngest there, most of the presents were for me. Amy had made me a beautiful dress and a patchwork quilt for my sister. Father had made me a rocking chair and a small crib for my new sister. Mother gave me all the bedding and some baby clothes for my sister. She must have made them in the fall before she got so sick.

"Hey Ellen, look here! There's a Christmas gift from Eaton's," my Father said.

I quickly grabbed the package and tore it open. My heart was pounding. I was very sad when I saw the gift. It was a doll that looked like the baby in the catalogue.

"But I wanted a real sister," I said. "This is only a doll."

"Oh, but think of the fun you can have learning about babies with this doll," Mother said.

I tried not to show my disappointment but I don't think I fooled anyone.

Mrs. Hogan and Amy went out into the kitchen to fin-

80

ish preparing dinner. Mother returned to her room where she went to bed to rest.

Mr. Hogan and my father carried on a conversation while I played with my new doll. It was kind of pretty with its frilly pink dress and bonnet. The dress matched my dress that I wore to the school concert.

Amy called us for dinner. We all joined hands and Father said grace asking God to bless all who were at the table. I ate lots of turkey and mashed potatoes and gravy. I did not like the cranberry sauce. Amy and I had picked the berries in the summertime and Mother had made the sauce and preserved it in jars.

"Your perogies are delicious," Mrs. Hogan said.

"Ellen made the filling," Amy replied.

I was so stuffed with the dinner that I wondered how I would find room for Christmas pudding and sauce. I did.

Mother excused herself and returned to her room. Mrs. Hogan, Amy and I did the dishes and cleaned up the kitchen.

Father and Mr. Hogan took coffee and went into the living room. We joined them and visited with them for the afternoon. At four o'clock they left so that they would be home before dark. Clouds were gathering again and it looked like more snow was on the way.

I scratched a peep hole in the frost on the window and watched the Hogans leave. A few flakes of snow were falling.

Merry Christmas Ellen. We know you have had a good day. Be happy!

Chapter 9

"ELLEN, HAVE you been reading and keeping up with your studies?" Mother asked.

"Yes."

"I am going to ask you some questions," Mother said. "What is the capital of Canada?"

"Ottawa."

"What province is Ottawa in?"

"Ontario."

"Who is the Governor General of Canada?"

I did not know the answer.

"The Governor General of Canada is the Duke of Devonshire, who is Victor Cavendish. He is the King's representative in Canada." Mother, Amy and I were sitting at the kitchen table having a little talk as we often did when we had a morning break. Father had gone into Pearl to get some lumber and building supplies. After the break Mother excused herself and went to her room. Some days she felt better than on other days. Today she was up early and feeling much better than usual.

Father returned from town and put a letter on the table that he had picked up at the post office. It was addressed to Mother and Father. There was no return address on the envelope but it had a Regina postmark.

"Who could that be from?" I asked.

"I don't know," Father replied. "I don't recognize the handwriting."

"Can we open it?"

"No," Father replied. "We should wait for Mother to read it with us."

I was very curious about the letter and kept hoping that Mother would come to read it. Amy was preparing Mother's dinner to take to her room.

"Amy, can you tell Mother about the letter?" I asked.

"Sure."

When Amy returned from delivering Mother's tray, I asked, "Will she come and see the letter?"

"Not right now Ellen. Maybe later this afternoon. But don't get too excited as she will not read it until your father is here. That will probably be after supper."

I was disappointed but I would just have to wait. Sometimes waiting was hard.

The time did finally come when we were all at the kitchen

83

table in the light of the kerosene lamp.

Father opened the letter and read it to us.

JANUARY 4, 1921

Dear Mr. and Mrs. Stover,

I don't know if you remember me but my name is Martha Hogan. I am the daughter of Jack and Elsie Hogan. I am Amy Stanford's friend.

Sometime ago I was sent to the convent in Regina to become a nun. While I did spend some time at the convent, I have since left and I am working in a restaurant here in the city.

I understand that Amy is living with you. I would like to see her again but it is just not possible for me to return to Pearl. We have much to talk about.

Amy was very fortunate to be able to live with you. I wish that I had known that people like you existed. You will be rewarded for your good deeds.

I hope that Ellen is fine and doing well in school.

I hope that you had a great Christmas and that you are all blessed in the New Year.

I am including an envelope addressed to me

in Regina if Amy would like to write to me. I
hope that she will.

Yours truly,

Martha Hogan

Amy's face had softened and a tear rolled down her cheek.
She choked as she said, "I'm so glad to hear from Martha. I've
thought about her a lot."

Father handed her the letter and said, "I think you should
have this."

"Oh thank you Mr. Stover. I will write Martha a letter
tonight."

We talked about how cold it had been and that Mother was
often cold in her bed during the day. The wind just seemed to
whistle right through the house.

After she went to bed we rearranged everything in the
kitchen and moved the couch from the living room. We set
it near the kitchen stove so that Mother would be warm. She
could spend more time with us as well.

The next day it was forty below Fahrenheit.

Father asked, "Ellen, would you like to come to town
with me?"

"Yes Father."

"Bundle up well as we will be riding in the open on the
wagon."

That would be a cold ride, but I was sick of staying home. I put on my leggings that were heavy long stockings with an elastic strap that held them over boots or shoes. They were long enough to cover my knees. I put on my ankle length red coat and bonnet that were made of a heavy flannel like material. I wrapped a scarf around my face exposing only my eyes.

Amy had heated some stones in the oven that we could put under our feet. Father had a scarf wrapped around his head. We each had a blanket that we wrapped around us before we left on our journey.

Father did not tell me where we were going with the wood; I thought it was for the school.

As we neared Pearl I looked at the red ½ painted on the sign and wondered who had done it. Some thought it might be Bubblin' Bob as he liked to play jokes on people. The residents of Pearl referred to the mystery painter as the Red Writer.

We pulled up to Betsy's house and Father went to the door and knocked. Mrs. Connor opened the door a crack and they exchanged words. I was too far away to hear what they were saying.

Father came back to the wagon and said, "Go into the house and warm up."

Betsy was wrapped in a blanket shivering when I came in. She said they had run out of wood during the night and she was very cold. I went outside and told Father that they needed wood right away. Father took a minute and made some kindling to help the fire get started. I hurried back to the house.

Mrs. Connor was in tears as she took the kindling and the wood that I brought. She had paper in the stove and she placed the kindling on top of the paper. She struck a wooden match and the paper caught on fire. The flames ignited the kindling and then the log was set on fire. I went outside and brought in an armful of wood for them to add later.

Mr. Connor was sitting at the kitchen table wrapped in a blanket. He was drinking beer. "Who are you?" he asked.

Betsy was quick to reply, "This is my friend from school, Ellen Stover. Her father brought us some wood."

He just grunted and took another drink.

Mrs. Connor heated some water on the stove. "Come and have a cup of warm water."

She made coffee. Later she offered my father a cup. I knew he was glad to get out of the cold for a while.

Betsy and I chatted about going back to school soon. They had a very quiet Christmas. Betsy showed me her Christmas present. It was a pretty blue sweater that her mother had knit.

"Come Ellen, we need to head for home," my father said.

I said good-bye to the Connors and we headed for the post office. Father mailed Amy's letter before we headed for home. I was really glad to see our house as I was really cold. The sky was very clear; there was not a cloud to be seen. The air was sharp and crisp.

"Oh Amy," I said as I came into the kitchen. "Betsy lives in such an old house. It is so cold and ugly. They had no wood."

"Goodness," Amy replied. "That must be awful."

"Why doesn't Mr. Connor work?" I asked.

"I don't really know."

"I don't think they have any food either."

"Why do you say that?"

"Mrs. Connor only gave us warm water to drink and Father got coffee."

Mother was resting on the couch and had heard our conversation. "Amy, the next time Henry goes to town, send a box of food with him, stuff that the cold won't hurt like dried beans, bread, butter and some baking if we have any."

"Yes, Mrs. Stover. I'll be glad to do that."

Father came in and got a cup of coffee and some coffee cake. I know that he was very hungry as he had missed his morning lunch.

"Ellen, I hope you are thankful for the food and the warm home that you live in," Father said.

"Yes. I really feel sorry for Betsy. Why doesn't her father work?"

"Mr. Connor is full of demons from drinking. It is such a waste of human life."

"I know why Betsy couldn't bring anyone home with her," I said. "She must be so ashamed living there."

Amy spoke up, "I could very well be in a situation like that. I thank God every day for both of you, Mr. and Mrs. Stover, and you too, Ellen."

"You more than earn your keep, Amy," my mother said.

"Yes you do," my father added.

"How long will this cold weather last?" I asked.

"I'm not sure," Father replied. "As long as it stays clear and cold we won't be getting any more snow for a while."

That was all right. We had enough snow. I busied myself with my knitting. I was still working on the blanket for Annie. Mother had insisted that I finish it. I had ten more squares to knit before I could sew them together.

My thoughts kept returning to Betsy and the awful house that she lived in.

How did they stay warm? We had to sit right by the fire for warmth as the cold wind blew through the cracks in the walls. Why couldn't Mr. Connor fix them? Father always fixed things around our house.

"Ellen, can you set the table for dinner?" Amy's voice interrupted my thoughts.

"Yes, Amy, be right there."

Amy had made soup that was full of vegetables and rice. She served it with bread and butter.

"What kind of soup is this?" I asked.

Amy replied, "Vegetable."

"But there's rice in it."

"I guess you can call it vegetable rice then. Soup is just

89

soup. I just put the leftovers in a pot of chicken broth and call it soup. Do you like it?"

"It's yummy." Hot soup on a cold day really warmed me up. I asked for a second bowl.

Amy served some strawberry Jell-O topped with whipped cream for dessert.

After dinner Amy and I cleaned up the kitchen and she sat near the stove working on her patches for her quilt. She had lots of blocks sewn together and soon she would be putting the quilt on a frame to stitch the wool, the backing and the pretty patches together.

Amy would quilt for a while then she would get out her books and do her assignments. She had worked so hard that she would be completing her grade twelve by spring. Her instructor gave her high marks and encouraged her to continue her good work.

I picked up the dresser scarf that I was embroidering. It was stamped with roses and I was stitching them in a bright red. I was to finish this item and Mother would crochet a lace edging around it and then it would be packed away in my hope chest to be used when I married. That day seemed very far away.

Whom would I marry? No one from Pearl even wanted to talk to me.

I went to the window and scratched a peep hole in the frost. There was a soft feathery cloud just stopped in the sky.

Hello Ellen. All will work out well for you. Be thankful for your nice home and family.

Chapter 10

I WAS GLAD when school started in February. It was still very cold; the windows were still covered with frost and the wood stove barely kept the chill away. We often wore our coats during classes.

Amy had made me a new blue dress that was the same color as my eyes and I wanted to show everyone how nice it was. Only Betsy told me how pretty it was. It made me feel guilty because her dress was so worn and faded.

It was the last week in February and we all expected the chinook weather in from Alberta but this year it just didn't want to come. The chinook wind was warm and dry coming in from the slopes of the Rocky Mountains. When it came it would be warm enough to melt some of the snow. For about a week it would feel like spring had arrived, but we would have to wait a little longer this year. I got to see Betsy every day and

I would stop at her house now. She felt better because I knew about the home she lived in.

Mother's health was getting worse; Amy was by her side constantly. I tried to help Amy as much as I could. I made most of the suppers. Father and I ate first and then Father would sit with Mother while Amy had her supper. Father and Amy took turns staying with Mother during the night.

Early on Easter Sunday the twenty-seventh of March, Mother was up and dressed. "I would like to go to church today," she said.

Father asked, "Are you sure?"

"Yes, I'm sure."

Could Mother be getting better? She looked so nice.

At church we got a lot of strange looks when we went to our usual pew. It had been a few weeks since we had attended church. Today we had arrived at the last minute and the Millers were sitting in the pew in front of us and the Bakers were sitting in the pew behind us.

After the service the pastor said, "Nice to see you Mary."

Two other ladies from the congregation wished Mother well. She just smiled at them and said, "Bless you."

Mother was tired from her outing so she rested when we returned home. She joined us at the dinner table. It was so nice to be a family again.

That afternoon the Hogans paid us a visit. When they were getting ready to leave, Father said, "Come with me Ellen. Let's help Mr. Hogan bring the buggy to the house."

I bundled up and joined Father and Mr. Hogan and we went to the barn.

When the Hogans were boarded in their buggy, Mrs. Hogan said to Father, "I fear that this is the quiet before the storm."

Father replied, "I think you are right Elsie."

Elsie responded. "Look after yourself Henry."

What did Mrs. Hogan mean about the quiet before the storm?

Amy had come outside and was feeding Spot. She looked very sad.

When Father and I returned to the house, Mother was lying down on the couch. She was asleep so we quietly went into the living room. The living room was usually reserved for company but lately we had been using it a lot so that Mother could rest quietly in the kitchen.

The weather was warmer now and the frost no longer covered the window panes. I watched the Hogans ride in their buggy as they headed towards town. Some dark storm clouds were starting to cover the horizon.

I hope they make it back to Pearl before it starts to snow.

The clouds were restless and getting darker. I was getting a strange feeling.

There is trouble coming. Be strong, Ellen. Be strong.

Mother called to me, "Ellen, could you please come here?"

I went to her side and she took my hand and said, "Sit down beside me. You have been such a great joy for me; you have made my life complete. Look after yourself and always remember that I will be by your side no matter what happens."

93

"Yes, Mother. Are you feeling better?"

"I am having a good day today. Now, why don't you play checkers with your father?"

Mother smiled and closed her eyes. I knew she was tired so I brought the checker board to the living room and asked, "Father, would you like to have a game?"

Father had a strange far away look on his face and he did not respond right away.

"What did you say Ellen?"

"Would you like a game of checkers?"

"Sure, why not? Are you ready to get beat?"

"Maybe I just might let you win," I replied.

Father beat me two games and then he helped me win the third. This game had lots of challenge.

The rest of the day went quickly. We did our chores, had supper and then Mother said, "I would like to dance to the *Skater's Waltz*. Henry, may I have this dance?"

Father replied, "Yes, you may. Amy, would you tinkle the ivories for us?"

"Sure, Mr. Stover."

Amy began to play the song and even I had to glide to the soft, graceful music. "Father, will you dance with a teacup?"

Father and Mother were such beautiful dancers. Father could dance with a teacup filled with tea on his head and not spill a drop.

"Why not?"

I brought him a cup and saucer but I did not put anything

in the cup. Father placed it on his head and they continued to waltz around the living room. They looked so graceful.

The teacup never moved as they danced. It was a short dance but Mother was so happy; she loved to dance.

Mother returned to her bed and Amy and I served hot cocoa and cake before we went to our rooms.

I lay on my bed remembering the happy faces of Mother and Father as they danced around the room.

Thank you for this great day!

There was no school for a whole week now as on Good Friday we started our Easter break. The weather was so nice that I walked to town to visit Betsy one day and she returned the visit the following Friday which was the first of April.

"Ellen, we're moving away to Regina," Betsy said.

My stomach got a strange feeling. "But why Betsy?"

Betsy looked very solemn for what seemed like a long time, "April fool."

I had to laugh, "Let's find Amy and try and fool her."

Amy was busy helping Mother so we decided not to try and fool her right now; we went back outside.

"Maybe I should go home." Betsy said.

"Yes, Betsy. Mother has been quite sick again. See you at school on Monday."

"Bye," Betsy said as she headed down the lane.

"Bye."

Father was coming from the barn and he stopped to talk to Betsy for a minute.

"How are you doing Betsy?"

"Good."

"Does your mother need anything? Do you have enough wood?"

"Yes, thank you, Mr. Stover."

"Bye Betsy. See you soon."

"Bye Mr. Stover."

Father asked, "Did you have fun with Betsy?"

"Yes. She fooled me though."

"You have to be on your toes to keep up to that girl," Father said as he chuckled.

We both went into the house. Amy looked weary and Father said, "I'll sit with Mary for a while. Why don't you take a walk and get some fresh air?"

"Thank you Mr. Stover. I think I will."

Amy left and Father said, "Can you prepare supper?"

"I think so. There are some leftovers that I can warm up."

"Good. I think Amy is very tired and she needs some help."

Mother was very sick all weekend and by Monday morning both Father and Amy looked exhausted.

I kissed Mother good-bye and she said, "I love you Amy. Smile that pretty smile of yours. I will always be by your side."

"I love you too," I said as I forced a smile.

I was glad to get back to my studies but I found it very hard to concentrate. The children seemed extra rude today.

"Hey Pinky, are you learning any tricks of the trade from the prostitute?"

96

I learned a long time ago that it was a waste to time to respond to comments like that. It would only encourage more rude remarks. I put an invisible wall around myself to protect me from the cruel words.

When school was over Betsy and I headed for home. We said good-bye when a dark cloud appeared from no where.

Hurry home Ellen. Hurry home.

I started to walk and then run. As I was coming up the lane Father came out and took me in his arms, "Your mother has just passed away."

"No," I cried out and ran to the house.

Amy was sitting in a chair just staring out the window. A sheet had been drawn over Mother's head. I stopped. I was too numb to respond.

I love you Amy. I will always be by your side. How could this happen? Mother lied to me.

An invisible wall was forming around me as I sat in a chair beside Amy.

"Oh Ellen," she said. "I'm so sorry for you. Your mother was such a good person. She can rest now; she will not have any more pain."

"How will we live without her?"

"We will have to do our best. She has taught us well."

The rest of the day and the next day were very busy ones as we prepared for the funeral. Father had built the coffin and Mrs. Hogan and Amy lined it with straw covered by white cloth.

Mother looked at peace but she had become very thin.

The coffin was placed in the living room where we stayed and kept watch.

On Wednesday the sixth of April, 1921 the pastor arrived just before two in the afternoon and he gave a short sermon for Mother. Only Mr. and Mrs. Hogan, Betsy and her mother, Bob Jones, Amy and Mother's cousin and his wife from Regina came to see Mother off to her home in the heavens.

Everyone but the pastor came back to our house after Mother was placed in the family cemetery. Amy and Mrs. Hogan served a lunch for the guests. Father thanked Mr. Jones for digging the grave.

Mr. Jones just patted Father on the back and replied, "Any time Henry, any time."

Was that a tear that rolled down Mr. Jones' cheek? He quickly turned away and said, "I'll be on my way now."

Mother's cousin Sam and his wife Hilda would be spending the night with us so we all gathered around the kitchen table when Father spoke to me, "Amy will be going to Normal School to become a teacher. She will be living with Sam and Hilda in Regina."

"Oh Amy," I said. "Can't you stay here with us? I will miss you so."

Father replied for her, "Amy must move on with her life. It is not proper for a young lady to live in a home with a man that does not have a wife. She has suffered enough here in Pearl."

"Oh, Amy," I said. "I will miss you so. Will you come back to Pearl to be my teacher?"

98

"I don't think so Ellen. I will miss you too. Will you write to me?"

"Yes, I will." I went to the window to search for a friendly cloud. There were four great big fluffy clouds floating about the sky. They smiled softly at me.

Be brave Ellen. Be brave. We are taking care of your mother now. She is just fine.

Chapter 11

IN THE morning Amy, Sam and Hilda were preparing to return to the city. Amy gave me a big hug and said, "I will write to you when I get settled in Regina."

"I wish you didn't have to go."

"I will miss you Ellen, but it is time to move on."

Amy would be living with the Reeses and she would cook and clean for them to pay for her room and board.

Father handed Amy an envelope and said, "Here's a little something to help you with your studies."

"But Mr. Stover," she said. "This is far too much."

"You have earned every penny," he replied. "You took such good care of Mary for us. She wanted you to have it. Good luck with your studies."

"Thank you Mr. Stover."

They left and Father and I were on our own.

"Let's take a walk to the cemetery," he said.

"All right."

We walked in silence. It was only a short distance away. There were trees on the west and the north side protecting it from the cold winds.

"I think I will put a little bench here this summer," Father said.

"That would be nice."

"Do you think you can look after the grounds like your mother did?"

"I'll try. Who is in those graves?"

Each grave was marked with a single cross.

"This one is your brother's and the other one is your sister's." Father answered. "They were both stillborn. We did not want you to be unhappy about them so we never told you."

"What is stillborn?"

"It means that they died before they came into the world. They did not breathe at all."

"How sad."

"They are with their mother now and they will all watch over us. Let's go home now."

We left. Two friendly clouds followed us home.

We are sad for you Ellen. Look after your father.

I took Father by the hand and he squeezed mine. His eyes were filled with tears.

Be brave Ellen. Be brave. We are watching over you.

It was seeding time and Father would spend all day in the

fields. One day he came home very tired and said, "Ellen, I don't think you should be by yourself all day. I have talked to the Hogans and we all felt that it would be best if you went to live with them."

I started to cry, "But this is my home. I can take care of myself."

"I know Ellen, but it is not fair that you have to be alone and work so hard. You're not eleven years old yet. You will have a better life with them."

"But who will play with Spot?"

"He will just have to come with me out to the field and romp. He will be fine."

The next day at school I told Betsy that I would soon be living in town.

"Good," she said. "Maybe we can get together after school more often."

It was a good thought but it didn't fill that awful pain in my heart. Something was missing.

I needed my mother and I missed Amy. Anger started to build in me as I got mad at both Mother and Amy.

Why did you have to leave me? I could still live at home and enjoy my days in the country.

Saturday morning came and I gathered my clothes and personal things, Annie and all her things and Father loaded them all in the buggy.

At the Hogan's house Father gave me a hug and said, "Be good and don't give the Hogans any problems, Ellen."

He left brushing something from his cheek. Was it a tear?

Mrs. Hogan helped me unpack. She had fixed up a room really nice for me. She said, "You can have a bath and get cleaned up before supper."

They had a room that they called the bathroom. It had its own tub and washstand. It was summertime and everyone was expected to use the outhouse. In the winter they had a spot where a toilet would be brought in. It had a pail that went inside the toilet that could be removed and emptied daily.

I had a bath and Mrs. Hogan helped me to wash my hair. When I returned to my room there was a new dress waiting for me on the bed. It was pink, my favourite colour. I quickly put it on and went to the kitchen where Mrs. Hogan was.

"Thank you ever so much for the nice dress Mrs. Hogan."

"You're most welcome," she replied. "Now that you will be living with us, I think you should call me something other than Mrs. Hogan. What do you think?"

"Yes, I think that you are right. Can I call you Mamma?" I didn't want to call her Mother as that was what I called my real mother.

"That would be just fine. Would you like to call Mr. Hogan Papa? We will ask him at suppertime if he would like to be called Papa. Would you set the table for me?"

"Sure Mrs. Hogan — I mean Mamma."

Mamma showed me where the dishes and cutlery were and I set the table.

"You set a nice table Ellen."

"Thank you Mrs. Hogan, Mamma."

Mother had shown me how and Amy helped me if I forgot to do it right.

"Here comes Papa."

"Hello Jack. Ellen is here now and we were wondering if she could call you Papa. We have agreed that she will call me Mamma."

Mr. Hogan was a rough sort of a guy but he softened a bit and said, "I think that would be quite all right. Hello, Ellen."

"Hello, Mr. Hogan — Papa."

Papa replied, "It will be good to have a girl around again." Their own daughter Martha had left over a year ago to go to the convent in Regina.

After a big supper of meat loaf, scalloped potatoes, corn and cucumber salad, I helped Mamma clean up the kitchen. I was very tired and Mamma said that I could be excused and go to my room and rest. I was glad for that. I went to my room, checked on the sky and saw a few friendly clouds drifting by.

There was a new nightgown for me and I put it on and crawled under the nice feather tick. It wasn't long before I drifted off to sleep. The feather pillows were ever so soft.

Everything is going to be just fine. Remember to forgive, forget and move on. *I forgive you Mother. I forgive you Amy.*

The next day I attended the Catholic Church with the Hogans. I did not feel comfortable there as the priest spoke the mass in another language. I was always being told to sit, stand, kneel or make a cross. By the time church was over my head was spinning. Father George was introduced to me.

He shook my hand and said, "Welcome Ellen. We must get you started on your studies for First Communion."

I did not like the strange way he looked at me but I was expected to reply with my best manners, "Yes, Father George."

We had a nice Sunday dinner and then Mamma and Papa said that they were going to have a nap. I could do the same or play quietly.

"Can I go to the schoolyard and play with Betsy?" I asked.

"I don't think that is such a good idea," Mamma replied.

I did not ask why. I knew my place in life. Children were to be seen but not heard. I went to my room and lay down on the bed and watched the dark clouds gather in the sky. They looked like rain clouds. Everyone was saying that we needed rain for the crops and gardens. I drifted off in a troubled sleep. I woke up from a bad dream. I kept seeing Mother in her coffin.

On May tenth I received my first letter. It was from Amy. My father brought it and he stayed to have coffee and cake with the Hogans. I wanted to rush away to my room and read the letter but I knew that would be very impolite.

When Father left, I ran to my room and tore open the letter.

MAY 2, 1921

Dear Ellen,

I miss you and your family and the farm. City
life is so different. People seem to be moving so
fast and doing so many things. I have an extra
job where I work at a café cleaning up after it
closes. It will help pay for the books that I will
need to go to Normal school in the fall. I got
the job with the help of Martha Hogan. She
works at the café during the day. She has left the
Convent and lives in a small room at the back of
the café. She has had a very troubled life. Some
day we will both tell you about the problems
we had living in Pearl. We hope that you should
never have to deal with the things that happened
to us.

Be strong Ellen. Remember those talks that
your mother had with you and I?

How are you doing in school? Do you miss
your mother? I bet you do. She was such a nice
lady. God has a special place for her in heaven.
She will watch over you.

I hope that you and your father are both
fine.

Please write soon.

Love,

Amy

I gathered a pencil, some paper and an envelope from my personal things that I had brought from home. I began to write.

May 10, 1921

Dear Amy,

I was so happy when I got your letter. I am living with the Hogans now. Father thought it would be best for me. I miss the farm. I miss Mother. I miss seeing Father every day. I miss you Amy. My life is very strange now.

The Hogans are good to me and they have such nice things, but I miss the farm. I miss the outdoor life with Spot and I even miss milking the cow.

I do not have very far to go to school now and I get to see Betsy almost every day. She is glad that I live in town. She is doing really well in grade four. She is a smart girl and she is at the top of the class all ready.

I hope that you like your new home and your

new school. I wish you could come and visit me.

Love,

Ellen

I went to the kitchen and asked Mamma, "Will you mail this letter for me?"

She said, "Sure. I will mail it on Friday when I go to the store."

"Thank you, Mamma."

I returned to my room and gazed out the window. The sun was setting in the west and the sky was clear. There wasn't a cloud to be seen. Somehow the day was good and I could fend for myself.

All is well here. I'm talking to you my clouds wherever you are. Beware Ellen! Beware! There lies a wolf in sheep's clothing.

Chapter 12

MAMMA TALKED to me about studying the Catholic religion and taking First Communion. I didn't like the idea but I could not refuse because I lived in their home. I said I would so she made arrangements for me to meet with Father George after school on Friday. I dreaded the thought of having to meet with that man. He gave me the willies.

After school on Friday I went to the church office that was attached to the church.

"Hello Ellen. Sit down while I explain what you will be studying."

"Yes, Father George."

"When you take First Communion you will become a great lady in the Catholic Church. You will be blessed. You will be of great service to your Lord and to the church. I like to prepare my girls for this blessed event."

I was squirming in my chair. I could not look at him as his creepy eyes were staring all over me.

He continued, "When you take First Communion you will wear a white gown. As you study and learn you will wear a white gown so that you will always be reminded of your special day."

I was getting scared now as his creepy eyes seemed to pierce right through me.

He opened a door behind him and said, "You will find a white gown on the chair. Remove all your clothes and put the gown on. When you are dressed, tap on the door to the office."

I went into the room that must have been the priest's bedroom. The white gown was draped over a chair. This just didn't seem right to me.

Don't do it Ellen. Don't do it.

There was that voice in my head. Now I was really frightened. There was only one door from the room and that was back into the priest's office. I cannot disobey the priest. What do I do now? I must get my thoughts together.

My mother's voice came through loud and clear, "You must always be strong Ellen. When things don't seem right, they probably aren't. Be strong Ellen. Be strong."

I knew what I had to do. I tapped on the door. Father George opened it and demanded, "Why haven't you put on the gown?"

I tried to dodge past him but he caught me by the arm. I fell to the floor. I started to kick wildly and luck was with me. He received a kick to the groin and it made him back away with a painful expression on his face. I made my move; I was

110

out the door like a shot.

I ran and ran as fast as I could. My feet took me to Betsy's house. I could not go home because Mamma would question me. No one ever dared to disobey a priest. I knew that I was in deep trouble.

Be strong Ellen! Be strong!

Betsy was out in her backyard when I came running over there. I was almost out of breath.

"Ellen, what's wrong? You look awful."

"Promise not to tell anyone?" I blubbered.

"Whom would I tell?" she asked. "You are my only friend."

"Oh Betsy, the priest wanted me to put on this white gown and I got really scared. He gives me the creeps. I kicked him and ran away."

"That dirty creep!" she replied. "You did the right thing."

"But what do I tell the Hogans?"

"Nothing. You can stay here until it is time to go home."

"Thank you Betsy."

"Be right back."

She came back with a glass of water and a wet face cloth. The cool cloth felt good on my flushed face.

I stayed with Betsy until it was time to go home. When I returned both, Mamma and Papa were waiting for me. Papa was furious, "Why did you run out on your classes?"

"I was afraid," I sputtered.

"You must never disobey the priest again. I will make sure that you remember that lesson."

Papa took a wide leather belt and demanded that I put my bare bottom up over the chair.

He proceeded to beat me over and over again. I was heart broken. The pain was easier to bear than the embarrassment. I needed my mother.

"Now, go to your room," Papa screamed at me.

I did not look back. I headed straight for my room where I closed the door and went sobbing to my bed. I had never in my life been treated this way. I lay on the bed shaking and sobbing.

Be still Ellen. You have done the right thing. Sleep my child. Sleep.

It felt like hours later that I fell asleep. In the morning I was told by Mamma to get dressed and prepare to go with Papa to the priest's office.

My stomach started churning and I ran outside to throw up. Papa would not let me alone until I apologized to Father George. He almost dragged me to the church. I had to apologize; I cannot remember what I said.

"Come back after school next Friday and we will start again," the priest said. He had a big grin on his face.

"Yes, Father George," I replied looking down at my feet.

It was Saturday today so I didn't have to go to school. My butt was so sore that I could not sit down. I spent the day in much pain. The backs of my thighs were black and blue and swollen. I wondered if I should tell my father. I decided that I would not burden him with my problem.

On Sunday I had to attend Mass with the Hogans. There was no way that I could avoid it. The priest's creepy eyes seemed to glare at me continuously.

I tried to sit quietly in the pew but I was still very uncomfortable. At the end of the service when the priest shook my hand he held it tight for a long time, "See you Friday after school," he said as his eyes pierced right through me.

"Yes, Father George."

On Monday I told Betsy what had happened to me. We talked a lot about my problem that week. As Friday drew near, I was really becoming frightened, almost frantic.

Betsy, bless her heart, came up with a plan. She would go with me to the priest's office on Friday and insist that she wanted to take the classes with me. Betsy and her family did not attend any church so this came as a big surprise to me.

On Friday she came with me as planned. The priest was not sure what to do with Betsy but she got to stay. The next week I attended classes with the younger children. I could breathe easier for the moment. Betsy continued to come to the classes. We needed each other's support.

On the way home that day the clouds seemed to beam at me. *Well-done Ellen. Betsy is a true friend.*

At home Mamma was busy preparing supper. Betsy said, "Hello, Mrs. Hogan."

Mamma replied, "Ellen has work to do. Run along now."

Betsy turned to me and said, "Bye Ellen. See you tomorrow." There was a sadness about her.

"Bye Betsy. See you in the schoolyard."

I quickly changed my clothes and went to help Mamma in

the kitchen.

"How did things go at Catechism today?"

"It was all right."

"Is Betsy attending classes?"

"Yes."

"Don't you think you should be making some new friends?"

"Betsy is such a good friend. Most of the kids just laugh and make fun of us at school."

"Other kids would be your friends if you stopped seeing Betsy. Her father is a drunk and that does not make a good choice for a friend."

I was shocked that Mamma would even think such a thing.

"She is my only friend."

"I don't think you should bring her around to the house anymore."

I could not reply. It was just too much for me. How was I going to tell Betsy? My whole world was starting to fall apart.

When Mr. Hogan came home for supper, he had my father with him. Mrs. Hogan asked him to stay and join us for supper.

"Thank you Elsie. I appreciate that. I haven't had a good home cooked meal for a long time."

Father and Mr. Hogan had coffee at the kitchen table while Mamma and I cleaned up the dishes after supper. I wanted to talk to my father so badly. I walked with him over to the livery stable where he had left the horses.

"Mrs. Hogan said I can't play with Betsy any more."

Father stopped and he had a sad look on his face. He looked

at me and said, "Ellen, you are living with the Hogans now and you must abide by their rules. I'm sorry but that's the way things have to be."

Even my father had turned against me today.

"I got a letter from Amy yesterday and she was wondering why you hadn't answered her letter. Did you not write to her?"

"Yes, I did. I asked Mamma to mail it for me and she said she would."

Father got a strange look on his face as he handed me a piece of paper. "You best not tell Mrs. Hogan about this letter from Amy. It was sent to me."

I tucked the letter under the top of my dress.

"Hop up in the buggy and I will drop you off."

I joined Father in the buggy. We were silent all the way to the Hogans. Father gave me a hug and left for home. I slowly walked to the house and went to my room. I was alone today; even the clouds had deserted me.

But I had a letter from Amy. I took it out from its hiding place and started to unfold it when Mamma called to me, "What are you doing Ellen?"

"Nothing."

"Can you give me a hand in the kitchen for a minute?"

"Sure."

The letter would have to wait. I tucked it under my pillow and went to the kitchen. It seemed to take forever for us to gather things together for a bake sale that was to be held at the church tomorrow. Mamma had baked three kinds of cookies, an angel food cake and a jelly roll. She would have to make the frosting for the angel food cake in the morning so that it would be nice and fluffy.

Finally we had everything done and I rushed off to my room to read the letter.

JUNE 15, 1921

Dear Ellen,

I have not heard from you so I thought I would write again. Are you all right? Why haven't you written?

How is your father making out on the farm? I still like the farm much better than the city. What plans do you have for the summer holidays?

I work hard every day and it keeps my mind from thinking about all my problems. I can hardly wait to start school. It would be so nice to be teaching in a school.

We have been having nice sunny weather. Are you still watching the clouds?

Please write soon.

Love from,

Amy Stanford

I was surprised that Amy had not received my letter.
Tomorrow I will write Amy another letter and have my father mail it for me.

I got ready for bed and thought for a while before that
voice came back to my head.

We must forgive, forget and move on. Forgive! Forget! Move on!

It seemed like I had to do a lot of forgiving these days. Do
children do everything wrong?

In the morning after I helped Mamma take the baked goods
to the church, I returned home to reply to Amy's letter.

JUNE 25, 1921

Dear Amy,

I don't understand why you have not received
my letter. I wrote you a letter in May and asked
Mamma Hogan to mail it for me.

The Hogans are very good to me, but I still
miss the farm. I go to the Catholic Church with
them but I hate it. The priest asked me to put on
a white gown to study for my First Communion. I
did not like the idea and he got really mad at me. I
kicked him really hard and was able to run away. I
only told my friend Betsy about it.

Betsy comes with me to study at the church
now even though her family does not go to

church. The priest doesn't bother me when she comes. I hate him. He gives me the creeps. Is it a sin to hate a priest?

I think you should send my letters to my father. Bye for now. Write soon.

Love,

Ellen Stover

I put the letter into an envelope and addressed it to Amy. I put it in my pocket and headed off to the farm to find my father. I would have to hurry there and back so that Mamma didn't know I was gone.

I found Father in the barn and said, "Hello Father. Can you mail this letter for me?"

"Hello Ellen. Nice to see you. Is that a letter to Amy?"

"Yes."

"I have some stamps in the house so let's go put one on your letter and you can drop it in the mail box yourself."

"Thanks Father."

"Here are a few extra stamps for you. The next time you want to write a letter just put one on it and drop it in the mailbox."

I thanked Father for the stamps and hurried back to town and to the post office. I pushed the letter through a slot in the door before I hurried back to the Hogans. I hoped no one had seen me go by.

A few clouds were skipping about and having a good time. They were happy clouds.

Come skip with us Ellen. Have fun in the sun. Be happy!

Chapter 13

THE LAST day of school was Thursday, June thirtieth. I did not know what I would do for the summer holidays. On the farm there were always fun things to do. In town the children would meet at the schoolyard to play sometimes when they weren't needed to help at home. They wouldn't play with me anyway.

Both Betsy and I had passed to grade five. All of Betsy's marks were in the nineties. Mine ranged from seventy-five to ninety. I loved Arithmetic and that was always my highest mark. I hated History and Science; they were always my two poorest marks. The other two subjects were Spelling and Reading. During the year we were taught music and art but they were not considered subjects; they were done as special projects.

I was just an average student and I often was left wondering whether I had passed or failed a test. I probably could have worked harder at my studies as I spent a lot of time with my head in the clouds, but that became a way of survival for me.

Time was running out for me; I would have to tell Betsy that I couldn't see her anymore. I didn't know how I was going to tell her. My eleventh birthday was next Wednesday the sixth of July and I had asked her if she could come. She had said she would and now I would have to tell her that she couldn't come. I would not be having a party as no one would come. I was starting to wonder if my life would have to be spent all alone.

My eye spotted a little ruby throated hummingbird fluttering nearby. It was so tiny and cute all decked out in its red bow tie. Would he find another hummingbird to fight with today? These birds did not want anyone to invade their territory and they would often flutter their wings very rapidly to chase other hummingbirds away.

I saw Betsy at church on Sunday and told her to meet me in the schoolyard in the afternoon. I would have to tell her somehow. The priest with his creepy eyes kept looking at me. I was glad when Mass was over.

I had trouble eating my dinner as I was upset about seeing Betsy. I helped Mamma clean up the kitchen and asked if I could go to the schoolyard.

Mamma replied, "Yes, but stay away from that Connor trash."

I just said, "Good-bye. I'll be back at three."

It was such a nice sunny day but it didn't make me feel any better. In the schoolyard I sat on a swing and kept looking toward Betsy's house. She came out and skipped her way to the school.

"Hi, Ellen. It's such a nice day. Should we go for a walk?"

"No, Betsy. I need to talk to you."

"Are you having trouble with Father George again?"

"No. This is even worse."

I decided that I would just have to blurt it out, "Mamma says you can't come to our house anymore."

Betsy's face fell. The news was just too much for her. She turned around and ran towards her house.

"Betsy, please come back. I'm so sorry."

She did not look back. My world had now been totally shattered. There was not a bright spot anywhere.

My darkness was interrupted by Vera Eastman who came and sat on the swing beside me.

"Are you expecting anyone?" Vera asked.

"No," I replied. She must know that I only had one friend. "Why do you want to know?" I asked.

"I just wondered if you would like to come to my house some time this summer."

"I don't know. What would your parents say?"

"They say it would be fine now that Amy is gone."

"Just what exactly is wrong with Amy?"

"I'm not sure."

"Amy was really good to me and Mother. She helped us a

122

lot. She was my only friend for a long time."

"Do you mind if I stay here on the swing?"

"No."

Three o'clock was nearing so I left for home. I watched the clouds dart around the sky. They were not stopping for me so they couldn't settle the sick feeling I had in my stomach. I needed my mother.

At supper I asked, "Can I walk out to the farm tomorrow to see Father?"

"After you have done your chores you can go," Mamma replied.

I felt a little better. Maybe I would even see Betsy on my way to the farm.

After breakfast on Monday, I helped Mamma clean the kitchen and then I went to tidy up my room. When I had finished, I stopped in the kitchen where Mamma was washing clothes. She was using a scrub board and rubbing the cloth up and down over the wavy glass ribs that had been covered with bar soap.

"Can I go now?"

"That's may I go now?"

"May I go now?"

"Yes. Be home in time for dinner."

"Yes, Mamma."

"Make sure you tell your father to come for supper on Wednesday."

"All right."

It was a bright sunny day when I headed out to the farm. There was no sign of Betsy as I walked by her place. I wanted to stop but somehow I knew I couldn't. I started to walk a little faster to try to leave my troubles behind. They kept walking as fast as I was. One pale white cloud strolled by slowly.

Life is not always the way we want it. Be strong Ellen! Be strong!

Father was not in the yard nor was he in the house. The kitchen was an awful mess so I started to clean the table. I worked for over an hour before Father came in the house. He was surprised to see me but he smiled warmly and gave me a hug.

"What brings you here Ellen?"

"I just came to see how you were doing."

"I'm doing fine. Do you want to come with me to see your Mother's grave?" he asked.

"Sure."

"Let's take the rake and hoe with us."

We gathered up the tools and headed out to the cemetery with Spot at our heels.

The tulips had bloomed and they were starting to die down. The peonies in the background were in bud.

"Come Ellen, I will show you how to prune the peonies. You see how each flower stock has a large center bud and two smaller side buds. Well I cut the two side buds off."

Father removed a pocket knife from his pocket and proceeded to cut all the side blossoms off.

"But there won't be many blooms now."

"That's right, but the center bloom will grow much larger and it will fill in the empty spaces. If we leave all the blooms on, the plant just wants to bend down and touch the ground because the blossoms are too heavy for its stem."

I hated to see them cut. Father threw the buds over in the meadow where they would decompose in the grass.

"What time is it?" I asked.

"It's eleven thirty."

"I need to leave for the Hogans as Mamma is expecting me home for dinner."

"It was nice to see you."

"Mamma Hogan said to ask you to come for supper on Wednesday. Can you come?"

"Yes. I will come."

Father made no mention of my birthday. Did he forget? I knew he must have a lot of things on his mind but wasn't I important too?

We took the garden tools back to the house and I washed my hands before I said good-bye and headed back to town.

"Say hello to the Hogans for me," Father said as he waved good-bye.

"I will. See you on Wednesday."

"Bye now."

I felt better so I started to skip along the lane. The clouds seemed to be skipping right along with me.

The day sped by rapidly and after supper I went for a walk.

I was hoping that Betsy would be out and maybe I could talk to her. I was near the Catholic Church when I almost panicked. I did not want to be anywhere near the Creep. Betsy and I had decided that we would refer to the priest as the Creep. This was our secret.

When I turned around to go back home, I saw my father leave the priest's office. What was he doing there? I was going to call out to him when that voice came again. Was it the dark blue cloud speaking to me?

Be still Ellen. Let your Father be. He is taking care of things. Be silent.

I hid behind a large maple tree and watched as my father walked rapidly in the direction of Main Street. He disappeared around the corner and soon he was headed home in his buggy. The sun was setting in the west and I knew that I must get home.

I started thinking about my eleventh birthday. What would I get for presents? I mostly got new clothing, but it would be nice to get a special gift like a necklace or a fancy scarf.

Mother always made sure that I would feel extra special on my birthday. I think Father just let her look after things like that.

Wednesday arrived and Mamma was up scurrying around the kitchen, "I have lots of things to do today Ellen. It is your birthday so you are free to do as you please today. Enjoy yourself."

"Thank you Mamma. Are you sure that you don't need any help?"

"Yes Ellen. Now sit down and have your breakfast. Papa had to leave early this morning."

I sat down to a breakfast of scrambled eggs, ham and toast.

"I am going to the schoolyard," I said.

"See you at dinner time."

I walked slowly to the school. I kept hoping to see Betsy somewhere.

Vera's younger sister Ruth was on the swings.

"Hello Ruth," I said.

"Hello," came the reply.

"Can I join you?"

"Sure."

Ruth was only eight years old so she was just a little kid. We did not have anything in common.

"I heard you couldn't play with Pukey any more."

"You be quiet about that. Her name is Betsy and that's all you should call her. Have a little respect for your elders."

Ruth sat silently on the swing for a few moments, "But everyone calls her Pukey. Even my mother does."

"That doesn't make it right."

"I have to go now."

"Bye."

"Bye. See you later," she choked.

Ruth left. She seemed upset with me. She was only a little child and I didn't want to be mean, but I still considered Betsy a good friend even though I was forbidden to see her.

What did Ruth mean about seeing me later? Was she going home to tell her Mother what I said? Would Mrs. Eastman come over to the school and talk to me about upsetting Ruth?

That was a troubling thought as Mrs. Eastman had a sharp tongue and she had been known to bluntly say what she meant. I could be in big trouble if she decided to see Mamma.

I had a strange sort of feeling in my stomach as I worried about Mrs. Eastman. By late afternoon I decided that Ruth had not told on me and I started to feel better.

Papa arrived home after work with my father. I looked out the window and there were the Eastmans coming up the walk and right behind them was the Creep.

I am in big trouble now. Oh please go away everyone. Just go away.

When the knock came at the door, Mamma said, "See who's there Ellen."

I dragged my feet on the way to the door. I had to open it.

"Happy Birthday Ellen," everyone said.

I stepped back. I was shocked at the response.

"Ellen, where are your manners?" Mamma interrupted my thoughts.

"Oh, thank you. Come in."

We enjoyed a big supper and Mamma lit the candles on my cake and everyone sang *Happy Birthday*.

I was glad when supper was over as the Creep kept looking at me strangely.

Mamma said, "You girls can run along now. I will look after

128

the kitchen."

"Thank you Mamma."

"Thank you Mrs. Hogan."

"I'll give you a hand," Mrs. Eastman said.

Around seven-thirty we all gathered in the living room and I was allowed to open my gifts. The Hogans had given me a new white dress with pink ribbons and a pair of fancy white shoes.

The Eastmans gave me a pink scarf. The Creep gave me a bookmark that was in the shape of a cross.

I thanked everyone for their nice gifts.

My father did not have a gift for me.

When everyone left, Father asked me to walk with him to the livery stable. On the way he gave me two dollars and told me to get myself something special. I gave him a big hug.

"Thanks Father."

"Ellen, I swear that your smile lights up the whole world. Here is a letter for you. Best you don't tell the Hogans about the money or the letter."

The letter was from Amy. There was just a little bit of light left when I opened it in my room. It was a birthday card that she had made for me.

Roses are red, Violets are blue, Happy Birthday, Ellen. I sure miss you.

What a nice verse. The clouds were gently floating about in the sky.

What a beautiful day you have given me! Thank you! Thank you!

Chapter 14

PAPA CAME home for supper all upset, "Someone beat up Father George on Monday."

"Oh, no," Mamma responded with a startled look on her face. "Who would do such a thing?"

"I don't know," Papa replied. "But I hope they find him and fix him good. Doc had to stitch him up."

I was starting to be afraid for my father. *Did he do it? He had no reason to go to the priest's office.*

"Does Father George know who did it?" I asked.

"He said he didn't know the man."

I breathed a sigh of relief. Father George knew my father so it couldn't have been him. I still wondered why he was at the priest's office.

"Father George is all right now but he needs to rest," Papa continued. "There will be no Mass for at least two Sundays."

That made me happy, but then I started to feel guilty.

Was it a sin to be glad that the priest was hurt? Was it a sin to be happy that I didn't have to go to church and see that creep for a while?

As I prepared for bed that evening the thought of my father leaving the priest's office kept coming back to me. A dark black cloud was moving in from the west. It got darker and darker and darker.

Should I ask my father why he was at the priest's office on Monday? Did he beat the priest? Was the priest afraid to say it was my father? My father was a big strong man, much stronger than the priest. Was the priest threatened?

There were so many unanswered questions. Then the voice came again.

Do not question your father. Let things be. He has taken care of things.

I fell into a troubled sleep. Betsy's birthday was next week on July the fifteenth and I wanted to see her so badly.

The next morning I took fifty cents from the money that my father gave me for my birthday and I went to the General Store. I purchased a blue scarf and left the store and headed for Betsy's house. I did not follow the streets but cut through some bushes. I knocked on the door. Mrs. Connor answered my knock.

"Can I see Betsy to wish her a happy tenth birthday? I am early but I want to see her."

"No, just please go away."

"Would you give her this scarf?"

"Yes. You better go now."

Mr. Connor let out an awful scream. Mrs. Connor closed the door and I had to leave. I returned home and spent a long troubled day.

The next week I meet Vera Eastman in the schoolyard at the swings.

"Pukey has moved to Regina," she said.

"Stop calling her that," I screamed at Vera. "Her name is Betsy."

"I'm sorry Ellen. I didn't mean to upset you."

"Betsy's father passed away and her grandparents came to get her and her mother."

"Poor Betsy," I said. "I hope she has a better life now."

"I hope so too," Vera replied. "We really didn't do anything to welcome the Connors here."

"I hope Betsy can forgive, forget and move on."

"Me, too."

We both left the swings and headed our separate ways with our separate thoughts.

Please take care of Betsy.

Late that afternoon Papa came in the house all out of breath and asked Mamma to come outside.

She went with him and they both came back very sad. Mamma was crying.

Papa said, "Ellen, we have something we have to tell you."

I waited with fear in my heart.

"Your father has died in an accident on the farm. He will be joining your mother in heaven," Papa said.

Mamma put her arms around me and just held me. I was too numb to move. This was just too much for me to take. I slipped out of her hold and fell to the floor.

I was in bed with Mamma calling me, "Ellen, Ellen, please wake up."

"I'm awake," I said.

"Thank goodness," Mamma replied. "You fainted dead away."

Dead, dead. Thoughts came rushing back. My father is dead.

I lay there unable to move.

"You rest now Ellen."

With that Mamma left the room and I was alone, numb and unable to put my life back to any sense of being normal again. Then the voice came again.

Rest, Ellen, rest. Your body and mind are tired. Rest, rest, rest.

And rest I did. I slept around the clock and it was seven o'clock the next day before I woke up. My body felt good. I wished that I could say the same for my mind. I got out of bed and headed for the bathroom.

When I came into the kitchen Mamma said, "We will be going to the farm right after breakfast. Your father has been prepared and Mr. Jones is with him now."

When we got to the farm Bubblin' Bob greeted us.

"I'm so sorry little girl," he said.

I did not know what to say.

"I found your father in the field and his leg had been cut by the plow."

Plop! Plop!

It sounded like the rain dripping through the roof and into the pot that collected it.

Plop! Plop! The noise didn't stop. It was not raining. Where was that noise coming from?

There it was. Blood was dripping from Father's coffin into a bucket beneath it. I immediately got sick and threw up. Mamma brought me a basin and then she went to get me a glass of water. I sat down on the couch and was sick again.

Plop! Plop! Plop!

It wasn't going to stop. I would have to get used to the sound. Father needed me.

Late that day Sam and Hilda Reese and Amy arrived. I was so glad to see Amy.

"Hello Ellen," Amy said. "I'm so sorry for you. How are you doing?"

I just sobbed.

Amy hugged me and said, "Everything will be all right. Your father can be happy again with your mother. Let him rest in peace."

Somehow that comforted me. I knew he missed Mother terribly. I did too. He could be happy now and I would be strong to make them both proud of me.

"Come Amy. We must prepare for the funeral."

We cleaned and baked and did the chores with the help of

Mr. Jones. When I was cleaning the table there were some letters and papers that I gathered up and tucked inside the top of my dress. I would deal with them later.

Father was buried beside Mother in the little cemetery. Mr. Jones had dug the grave. On the way back to the house Amy pointed to the sky.

"See that cloud over there Ellen? I think it has a smile just for you. I bet that is your mother watching over you."

And so it was.

Be strong Ellen. Be strong. We are here when you need us.

When we returned to the house there was a strange man waiting for us. He said that his name was Peter Morley and that he was a lawyer that lived in Pearl.

Was he the man they called Pick Pocket Pete?

"Is there a Sam Reese here?" he asked.

"I'm Sam."

"I need to speak with you."

Sam and Mr. Morley sat at the table on the veranda while the rest of us went into the house to serve lunch. We could hear them talking.

"Henry made a new will just two weeks ago," the lawyer said. "He has named you as Ellen's custodian. There is money for her care."

I wasn't sure what custodian meant so I asked Amy.

"That means I will have to come to Regina and live with you?"

"Yes," Amy replied.

135

I almost welcomed the news.

"But what about the Hogans?"

"They will learn to live without you," Amy replied. "That shouldn't be too hard for them. They were able to live without Martha."

The lawyer came into the kitchen and asked, "Ellen, do you know where your father buried his money?"

I was about to answer yes when something stopped me.

Say no Ellen. Say no.

I replied, "No."

The lawyer returned to the veranda and said, "We may have a little problem here. I will sell the livestock and send you some money just as soon as I can."

"That will be fine," Sam said.

When the lawyer left I said that I would like to return to the cemetery for a short time. I hurried off. The grave had been covered and a big pile of dirt lay on top of it. The mound on Mother's grave had been that high when she was buried, but it was smaller now.

Somehow it reminded me of the world around me. It was getting smaller and smaller.

I sat down on the bench and looked around to see if anyone had followed me. There was no one in sight. I lifted the cross from my brother's grave and pulled out a tin from the hole. I opened it and there was a big roll of money in it. I carefully placed the paper money in the legs of my bloomers. My bloomers were under pants that hung almost to my knees. They had elastic in the bottom of the legs so that they fit snugly.

There were a lot of coins as well. I left them in the tin as they would make too much noise if I took them. I returned the tin to its hole and replaced the cross and packed the soil around it.

When I returned to the house Papa was talking to Sam.

"Come along Ellen. We must go home now."

I said good-bye to everyone and Sam said, "We will pick you up at seven in the morning Ellen."

"It was your father's wish that you live with the Reeses," Papa said.

We boarded the buggy and left for Pearl. I took one last look at the home I had once loved so well. Would I ever see it again?

A soft cloud puffed its way across the sky.

Keep moving Ellen. Keep moving. You will move on to a better life.

Chapter 15

EARLY THE next day the Reeses came to pick me up. Mamma had packed my clothing and personal things in two boxes. They were put on the floor of the buggy. Papa helped me into the buggy and I sat beside Amy with my feet on a box. We said good-bye to the Hogans and we left for Regina. As I looked back at Pearl, the sign with ½ on it caught my eye. Would they ever learn who the Red Writer was?

We would have to spend the night on the road as the trip was too long to make in a day. Hilda had packed food for the trip.

When we arrived in Regina I hated the city immediately. The houses were placed so close together that there was hardly room to walk between them. The Reeses home was no different. Theirs was a large two story white house with green trim. I felt that I was encircled or jailed. There was no room for anything. There was not much to see but houses and houses and more houses. Hilda had a small garden in the backyard and flower beds all around the house. Snapdragons were still in full bloom flashing their yellows, oranges, reds and pinks. They were a welcome sight as a hummingbird hovered over them.

The Reeses had no children so they really didn't know what to do with me. They said that I could call them Sam and Hilda. That seemed very strange to me as adults were called either Mr., Mrs. or Miss. Life was going to be very different here.

While Hilda showed me to a room that was to be mine, Amy was in the kitchen preparing supper. Sam had left to return the team and buggy that he had rented from the livery stable. I remembered that I had brought some papers with me that were on the kitchen table at my home on the farm. I found them and started looking through them. There was a letter addressed to Father.

JUNE 27, 1921

Dear Mr. Stover,

Amy has talked to me about your daughter Ellen's situation. I, too, fear for her safety. The priest harmed me as well. I was sent to the convent to give birth to his child. I was just too small and weak to fight him off.

Please watch out for Ellen.

Respectfully yours,

Martha Hogan

This news was very upsetting to me. The Hogans had sent their daughter away because of that stupid creep. At least Amy had a home with us.

Why did adults always accuse children of being in the wrong? Children are so small and can't defend themselves.

There were two more pages in the letter. One was a letter addressed to my father from Amy and the other was a letter addressed to me from Amy.

June 27, 1921

Dear Mr. Stover,

I am writing to you because I am very concerned about Ellen. Do you remember the day that I came to stay with your family? Well, you will remember my story. Ellen has told me that the priest attempted to harm her but she was able to get away. I fear for her safety.

Martha Hogan has enclosed a short letter.

I am also enclosing a short letter for Ellen. I fear that my letters will not get to her unless I send them to you. Please give it to Ellen.

The weather is very nice here. The Reeses are good to me. I do work long hours but it helps to fill in the time before I start school in the fall.

Respectfully yours,

Amy Stanford

Had that creep harmed Amy as well? Why did the Stanfords disown her? Amy had never really told me.

JUNE 27, 1921

Dear Ellen,

I have sent this note to your father so that you would be sure to get it. I am just fine. I see Martha quite often now. She has a boyfriend and he seems nice.

Be strong Ellen. I know that you will have difficulty attending church. Just keep Betsy by your side and you will do fine.

Enjoy your summer holidays.

Love always,

Amy Stanford

Amy did not know that Betsy was now living in Regina. I just never told her as everything had been turned upside down the last while. I would tell her later.

After supper I helped Amy clean up the kitchen. She had to go to her job at the café and I was left to entertain myself. I went to my room and sat in a chair that was covered with a cushion that matched the bed covers.

When Amy came home from work, she tapped on my door.

"Come in," I said.

"I've just come to say good night."

"Oh Amy, I just read your last letter. It was with Father's papers. Betsy's father passed away and they moved to Regina."

"That's too bad. Maybe Betsy will have a better life here."

"I hope so."

Amy left and I lay down on the bed and I was so tired that I dropped off to sleep right away.

In the morning Amy was making breakfast. It was her job to cook the meals and clean up after eating. I helped her by setting the table after she showed me where everything was. After breakfast we cleaned up the kitchen and dusted furniture in the living room.

Hilda told me that I was expected to keep my room clean and tidy at all times. I was to make the bed and sweep the bedroom floor every day. I soon got in the habit of doing my chores right after breakfast and normally my work was done by eight o'clock in the morning. Sam was gone to work at the sawmill by then and Hilda was usually out in her garden.

One morning Amy was mixing up a batch of bread and I came to watch her. Later when the bread was ready to put in pans she let me help her. We had fresh bread for dinner that day.

"Do we need any supplies for the kitchen?" Hilda asked Amy.

"No."

Milk was delivered to the door every day. Money was left in a milk jar with a note saying what they wanted for that day. The milkman made his delivery before six. Mail was also delivered to the door and put in a mailbox that was mounted on the railing of the veranda.

When Hilda left, I decided that I needed Amy's help with the money I was carrying around in my bloomers. I kept it there in the day time and I put it under the mattress when I went to bed at night.

"I have a whole lot of money that I keep in my bloomers. I got it from Father's tin that he buried in the ground. What should I do with it?"

Amy said she would help me count it and then we would decided what to do with it. When we were done counting, Amy said there was more than three thousand dollars.

"You're rich Ellen. I think we had better keep this our secret," she said.

143

Women seldom had any money as these matters were tended to by the men. In fact, any money that a woman possessed had to be given to her husband or to a male adult that was responsible for her care.

Amy found a tin and put the money in it, all except ten dollars.

"Put this ten dollars in the special pocket that is sewn in your dress. That way you will always have money if you should need it."

I did as Amy said and then we went out to the backyard to find a place to bury the tin. Amy showed me a spot right next to the foundation of the house on the north side. "I will dig it in there for you but I will have to wait until after dark to do it."

I was glad that Amy was there to help me.

Hilda came home with three new dresses for me to wear to school. They were so beautiful all covered in fancy lace.

"But they are too nice to wear to school," I insisted.

"No, Ellen. You live in the city now and you must dress like the city children. I don't want the children to make fun of you."

I remembered how the children of Pearl had tormented Betsy about her shabby clothes. I did not want any part of that. But how would I play ball or swing or chase gophers in such clothes? I would have to wait and see.

We were soon all gathered at the supper table. Amy and I cleaned the kitchen and she left to clean the café. When she came home from work, the sky was dark with rain clouds and she was able to bury the tin with money. It started to rain just as she had finished.

In the morning I went to the backyard and the rain had made mud of the soil and it hid the place where Amy had dug to bury the tin.

It was Saturday and everyone was expected to have a bath in the evening. Here there was water that came from a tap. It was cold but hot boiling water was added to make it comfortable and when you were done you just pulled the plug and let the water go through a hole in the tub. I don't know where it went but it sure beat emptying the tub by the pail. We did not have to share the bath water. Each of us had our own.

Sam and Hilda were going to play cards at a friend's house and Amy went to work.

"If someone knocks at the door, do not answer it," Hilda said to me. "Keep the door locked at all times after we leave."

"Why?"

Nobody ever locked their doors in Pearl. If someone got caught in a snow or rain storm they were welcome to use your home even if no one was home. Why didn't people in the city do the same?

"Sometimes there are some bad people looking to rob or take advantage of you. Just keep the door locked."

That didn't sound very good to me. It was just another reason for me not to like city life.

On Sunday we all attended the Lutheran Church. I was glad

145

to be back in the old familiar routine. It was a large church with a big congregation. The pastor announced that they would be starting Confirmation classes in September. I would have to attend if I wanted to become a member of the church.

After the sermon was over Amy said to me, "I would like to join in the classes. Will you be going?"

"Yes."

"I haven't been going to church since I came to the city, but I feel that I want to go now."

"Good," I replied. "I will have someone to go with me."

When the pastor shook our hands at the door he said, "Welcome Amy and welcome Ellen. We would love to have you attend our classes. Amy, if you work really hard, you can be confirmed next June."

I would have to attend for two years because I was younger. Older people were often confirmed in one year or less.

Sam suggested that we take a walk around the area so that he could show me where I would be attending school. It was a sunny morning and we walked slowly through the streets. Sam or Hilda would comment on some of the buildings. They did not know who lived in the houses. This was rather strange. In Pearl we knew who lived in every house. We also knew every dog, cat and horse that belonged to the town.

When we reached the school, I was surprised to see how big the building was. This was no one room school.

"My goodness," I exclaimed. "How many children go to a school like this?"

"I'm not sure," Hilda replied.

"Each grade is in a room by itself and each grade has its own teacher," Amy added.

I could not imagine all those students and teachers in one building. I was afraid that I would get lost.

There was another group of people heading our way. There was a girl about my age and a woman, probably her mother and an older couple. As they came closer, I got a strange feeling. Could it be?

"Amy, is that Betsy Connor?"

"I believe it is."

I walked over to the group and there she was.

"Oh, Betsy! It's so good to see you."

"Ellen, is that really you?"

"Yes."

Soon we were hugging and dancing around. All of the past hurts were gone; it was just too great a friendship to toss away.

Betsy said she would be attending this school. We introduced everyone. Betsy was with her mother and grandparents. Betsy said they lived nearby and they cut through the schoolyard on their way home from church.

"Well, everyone, I think it's time to head for home," Sam said. "I'm getting hungry. Nice meeting all of you."

We said our good-byes and departed, each going in the opposite direction. I felt better. There were no clouds in the sky today, but I knew they were somewhere listening to my good news. Having Betsy back in my life just made everything seem so much better.

It is a very good day!

Chapter 16

I WAS SO happy about seeing Betsy that I thought I would share my news with Vera in Pearl.

JULY 19, 1921

Dear Vera,

I am so excited. Today after church we went for a walk to the school. It is so big. Amy tells me that there is a room for every grade and each grade has its own teacher.

While we were there, I saw Betsy Connor. She will be going to the same school.

How are things back in Pearl? It is a nice sunny day here.

If the priest asks you to put on a white gown, don't do it. Kick him if you have to. Just don't put on that gown.

Please write back. I will print my return address on the envelope.

Sincerely,

Ellen Stover

I was careful to date the letter for Monday because Mother said it was disrespectful to date a letter on Sunday. I addressed the letter to Vera being careful to put my return address on the envelope in the upper left hand corner. I sealed the envelope and put it on the dresser. I would have to get a stamp; I did not know where the post office was. The mail was delivered to the door.

Why did I tell Vera about the white gown? She would surely wonder.

I went to the kitchen where Amy and Hilda were preparing supper. I set the table. Hilda said she had stamps and that the mailman would take the letter right here. She gave me a two-cent stamp and I placed in on the envelope.

The next day was a beautiful sunny day. I was waiting for the mailman to hand him my letter.

"Are you visiting the Reeses?" he asked me.

"Yes," I replied.

"Have a good visit."

As the postman continued on his way, I thought about the start of school. Amy would be starting Normal School. I thought about how Betsy and I would be treated at the new school. Then I remembered how worn Betsy's dress was. I had three beautiful dresses to wear to school. She would feel just awful and I was sure the students would tease her.

Hilda came outside to work in her flower beds. She spent a lot of time with her plants. She always had a bouquet of cut flowers in the house.

I went back into the house to do my chores. As I was helping Amy in the kitchen, I had a thought, "Amy, could we take some of my money and buy Betsy some new dresses for school?"

Amy said, "You're just like your mother. She would have done the same. She would be very proud of you for doing it too."

"Can you take twenty dollars from my tin and buy Betsy three new dresses?"

"Yes, but how do we get the dresses to Betsy? We don't know where she lives."

"She said she lived near the school and that they cut through the schoolyard on their way home. Maybe we could walk in the area and see her?"

"That just might work. Let's try this afternoon."

We found Betsy's house. Her grandfather was mowing the grass in the front of the house. We were careful not to let him know that we were there.

On the way home Amy said, "I will get the money after dark tonight and I will go shopping tomorrow. I will take the dresses to Martha's place. How should we give them to Betsy? It will probably make her feel bad if we just give them to her. Besides, her mother would wonder where we got the money."

"Can we wrap them up and address them to Betsy and stuff them in her mailbox after dark?"

"Good idea. I think that it's best that Martha and I deliver the parcel. That way Sam and Hilda will not suspect anything."

The plan was put into action and everything was done. I hoped that Betsy could have a much better year at school than she did in Pearl.

The rest of the summer went by very rapidly. School started on the sixth of September, the day after Labour Day. City schools opened earlier than the country schools. Most students were not needed to help complete the harvest. I met Betsy at the door of the school. We were both nervous and excited. We walked up the steps and entered the building. There was a long hallway with doors on both sides. We went to the left and started reading what it said on the doors. The grade number and the teacher's name were printed on the doors in large letters.

It appeared that we were headed in the wrong direction. We started back and it was not long before we found our room. Our teacher's name was Miss Rogers. We were all asked to take a desk and wait until the bell rang and then classes would begin.

152

The bell rang and Miss Rogers asked us all to rise and we sang *O Canada* and said *The Lord's Prayer*, just like we did at school in Pearl.

Miss Rogers then asked us each to stand and tell the class our names. There were thirty students, twenty boys and ten girls. When Betsy stood up, I noticed that she was wearing a green dress and she looked every bit as good as the other students.

We were given a scribbler, a pencil and a reader. It was strange having only one class in the room.

At recess time we were asked to go outside. Out in the schoolyard there were students everywhere. Some played ball, some played football while others just stood around.

Betsy and I ate our lunch together. I was glad to see that she had enough food as I remembered the times that I was sure she did not have enough to eat.

The first three weeks in September went by so fast. School was fun and we were busy with Confirmation classes and school projects.

Later that month a letter arrived from Pearl.

SEPTEMBER 19, 1921

Dear Ellen,

How are you? I am fine. Mother and Father are starting to talk to me about marrying Harold Smothers. He is thirty years old, has lots of money and would be able to take care of me. He would build me a nice house on the farm. I have only seen him in church and I don't know what to think. He looks so old.

Have you been going to school? I hope you have found some new friends and don't have to spend your time with Betsy.

Miss Walkerton still teaches here. I told her I got a letter from you. She told me to wish you well if I wrote to you.

We are all fine. Ruth is being a pest but that's Ruth.

Sincerely,

Vera Eastman

I was mad at Vera after reading that letter. I didn't know if I would even answer her. Betsy was my best friend and when she hurt my friend she also hurt me.

Ruth was a good girl and I'm sure she would be fine if she wasn't made to taunt Betsy and me.

I put the letter aside and thought that I should talk to Amy about it. Amy always seemed to know what to do.

I went to the kitchen to help prepare supper. The sun was much lower in the sky now, a sign that winter was not far away. There wasn't a cloud in the sky. It would be very cold tonight. I must ask for an extra blanket for my bed.

"Amy, Vera said something bad about Betsy and I don't know if I want to write back to her."

Amy replied, "I think you should stay in touch with a young person in Pearl. Some day you may need help and the adults just seem to look the other way."

I thought about that for a while and decided that Amy was probably right. I would write to Vera explaining to her that she must never say anything bad about Betsy or Amy again. They had been my friends when no one else would talk to me.

At school, Betsy and I were meeting other students. Our teacher assigned us to someone different to work on special projects. We both felt good about going to school. It looked like Betsy would be at the top of the class. I was happy for her. I was still an average student.

Hilda and Sam continued to treat both Amy and I well but they just didn't know how to raise children. They left us to ourselves a lot. Amy was much like a mother to me. She was doing well at Normal School; she would make a good teacher.

One day after school, Betsy asked me to stay at the school grounds because she wanted to tell me something.

We sat on swings and Betsy began to tell me some shocking news.

"Remember Father George?"

"Yes, the Creep," I replied

"Well," she continued. "After you said you couldn't play with me I started going to his office because I had no one else to talk to. We often didn't have enough food to eat and Father George would give us stuff. But I had to repay him with favours."

"Oh, no Betsy. What did he ask you to do?"

"I had to put on a white gown and wait for him on the bed. He did awful things to me. He said the Lord was blessing me."

"Oh, Betsy, I'm so sorry. It's all my fault."

"No, Ellen, it's not. I used to think so. Adults just get in the way sometimes."

"But how could your mother let this happen?"

"She didn't know. I told her that I was helping Father clean and tidy his office. I think she was just so grateful for the food that she didn't care where it came from. I know she went hungry many times so that I could have food."

"I'm so sorry Betsy."

"It's over now. Sometimes we do things that aren't right. I don't go hungry now and my mother seems to be able to provide nice things for me."

"Good."

We parted after I promised never to tell a soul. I crossed my heart and hoped to die if I broke that promise to her.

I must really take better care of Betsy so that she would always have nice clothes and food. The Creep could have given her food. He did not have to take advantage of a nine-year-old girl.

My life was full of so many secrets. I shared different secrets with different people. It was getting hard to remember who shared what with me.

I still wondered if my father had beaten the priest. No one knew for sure except the priest. I was not going to ask him.

Then there were the letters that Amy and Martha had written to my father. Should I let them know that I had read them?

Amy and I shared the money secret. I alone knew about the money back at the cemetery.

Is it right to have so many secrets? Does everyone have secrets like me?

A little cloud was stopped overhead.

You are a blessed child to have secrets shared with you. Do not let these secrets worry you. Be true to others.

Chapter 17

MY LIFE fell into a routine of work, school, church and visits with Betsy. Plans for Christmas concerts were well underway both at church and at school. We were asked to write a poem as part of our Literature class and the best three would be a part of the school concert.

"Amy, I have to write a poem this week," I said to her as we were preparing supper.

"Have you got anything started yet?"

"No. I'm having a hard time coming up with some ideas."

"Always write about something you know and understand. How about your life in the Christian community of Pearl?"

I thought about that for a moment, "Good idea. It brings some thoughts to mind."

After supper, I went to my room and prepared to put my thoughts on paper. It was easy to write about my life, but it was a door that was hard to open. I knew the poem would be titled *Forgive Forget and Move On*. These were my mother's words and I would dedicate the poem to her.

Forgive Forget and Move On
A poem by Ellen Stover
Dedicated to my mother Mary Stover
A rose now grows on your hill
A sign that you love us still;
And come each morn, it does shine
For all to see and give a sign
That you are here and never gone
For you still forgive, forget and move on.

Early in December another secret was told to me. We were in the middle of a big blizzard when a knock came at the door. I knew that I was supposed to ask who was there but it was cold outside and the visitor needed shelter. When I opened the door a young girl was there all covered in snow.

"Oh, Ellen I'm so glad to see you," the young girl said.

"Vera, is that you? Come in and get out of the cold."

She tried to brush the snow off her coat but it was so thick that it appeared to be impossible.

"Come in," I said. "We'll clean off the snow inside."

"Thank you Ellen."

Vera came in and I took her coat and shook the snow off. She removed her leggings. I took her coat, scarf, mitts and leggings into the kitchen and hung them on a line to dry by the stove. She was shivering.

"Come sit by the fire."

I pulled a chair over to the stove and opened the oven door. Vera sat down and I draped a blanket over her shoulders.

Hilda came out to the kitchen and I introduced her to Vera. Hilda made some hot cocoa and soon we were all eating coffee cake.

"How did you get to the city?" I asked.

"On the train."

"How did you find us?"

"I knew your address from your letters and I asked a person at the train station where Osler Street was."

"Did you walk here?" Hilda asked.

"Yes."

We lived six blocks from the station and it was such a blizzard that it was amazing that she had found us.

"What brings you to Regina?" I asked.

Vera squirmed in her chair.

"Have you run away from home?" Hilda asked.

Vera bent her head and nodded yes. Tears started to roll down her face.

"We will talk about this later when Sam comes home. Your parents must be worried sick about you. We must send them a telegram."

"Please don't do that," Vera begged.

I knew that Vera would need a place to stay, "Can Vera stay

160

with us tonight?"

"Yes, but I cannot promise anything else until I have talked to Sam."

Vera and I went to my room and I helped her unpack the few things that she carried in a small bag. Everything was wet from the long walk in the snow storm. I took the clothing to the kitchen and hung them on the line.

When I returned to my room, Vera said she had something to tell me.

She began, " Harold and I have made plans to be married in the fall of 1922 after the harvest is done. We have started taking marriage lessons with Father George."

Vera got all choked up and couldn't talk for a while. She continued, "Father George said he would have to talk with us separately. I went one day by myself. He told me that he would have to prepare me for my wedding night with my husband. He told me to take off all my clothes and put on a white gown and wait for him on the bed."

"Oh, no Vera. What did you do?"

"I remembered you writing that I shouldn't put on a white gown and to run away. It brought back all the bad memories of my Catechism days and I ran away."

"You did the right thing," I said.

"My father gave me an awful beating after the priest told him that I refused to cooperate at my lesson and that he could not marry us until I did. I went to the store and stole some money from the cash register. I got on the train and here I am."

I hugged Vera and said, "We must come up with a plan to keep you from having to see that creep again."

Sam would be home in two hours and we would have to have a plan by then. We could not disclose the story about the priest. Even though the Reeses were Lutheran, they would not take kindly to anyone disobeying a man of the cloth. Children were the responsibility of their parents and they would insist that Vera return to the Eastman home in Pearl.

We decided to tell them that she did not want to marry Harold as he was just too old. Vera was almost fourteen; it would be hard to convince them that they should accept this as a reason.

Girls at the age of twelve and thirteen were often married because their parents could not afford to feed and clothe them. They looked for a man that could take care of them. These men were often old enough to be their fathers.

It was not easy but we were able to persuade Sam and Hilda to let Vera stay for a while. Vera said she did not want to go back to school anymore and that she would find a job.

"I'll send a telegram to your folks tomorrow and let them know you are safe," Sam said.

"Thank you Mr. Reese and you too, Mrs. Reese."

Vera would have to share my room but that was fine with me.

Hilda gave Vera two of her dresses and some under things. She was a small woman so her clothes fit Vera.

I was burdened with yet another secret when Vera added this bit of information, "I think that Father George is making Ruth wear the white gown. She is taking Catechism now and

162

she is acting real strange."

"This is just not right," I said. "We have to stop that creep!"

"You know that his word is law."

"Yes, but I think I heard somewhere that laws can be broken."

"That sounds like something Pick Pocket Pete would say," Vera replied.

"I'm not sure."

Vera got ready for bed while I stood at the window looking for a cloud. There wasn't one available as they were still busy dumping large snowflakes.

This was just too much for me to bear. Why were all these secrets told to me?

I stood staring at the falling snow when that voice came from nowhere.

Be strong Ellen! You will come up with a plan. You are strong!

That night I fell into a troubled sleep. By morning I thought that I had come up with a solution to everyone's problems with the Creep. I would talk to Amy about my plan.

The next day Vera was able to get a job cleaning rooms in a hotel that was nearby. She would have to work six days a week. Sam and Hilda had agreed to let her stay with us until the New Year. She would then have to find a place of her own.

It was Friday and Betsy came to school looking all grown up. Her dark, long hair was pinned up in a bun on the top of her head. She was slim and starting to mature. We thought of it as "busting out".

"Betsy, are you wearing rouge?" I asked.

"Shhhh, not so loud."

"You are, aren't you?"

"Yes."

"Does your mother let you?"

"No. I snuck out of the house before she could see me."

I didn't think Betsy should be wearing rouge to school.

"Betsy, you will go to the bathroom and remove your rouge." Miss Rogers said. "And you must never come to school like that again or you will have to see the principal."

Nobody ever wanted to go to the principal's office because he would use the strap or a big ruler to punish you. When you got home you would be punished again by your parents or custodians. I did not want that ever to happen to me.

Betsy's face turned beet red and she quickly got up and left the room. I felt sorry for her because she had been embarrassed in the classroom. When she returned she quickly and quietly walked to her seat with her head down.

At recess Betsy said to me, "Please don't tell my mother."

"No, I won't," I said. "But please don't do that again."

My mother never wore makeup nor did she think it was a healthy thing to do. She often said that real beauty came from within, and if you had a kind and thoughtful heart beauty would glow in your cheeks and sparkle your eyes.

"You are beautiful just as you are," I said.

Betsy promised that she wouldn't wear rouge to school anymore. Sometimes I would see her put it on after she left the schoolyard. I decided that I would not talk to her about it as she would be in

164

trouble at home if she didn't take it off before she arrived there. Her grandparents would be horrified to see her like that.

The days were passing by and soon it would be the school concert. My poem placed third in the contest and I would be reciting it at the concert. I was quite nervous about doing that as there would be so many more students and parents in the audience than at Pearl.

A week before Christmas Vera showed me a letter that her sister Ruth had written to her.

DECEMBER 15, 1921

Dear Vera,

I miss you. It is so cold and I don't know what to do. The priest makes me put on this white gown and then he does awful things to me. I am afraid to tell anyone.

What are you doing in the city? How is Ellen?

Mamma and Papa would like you to come home. So would I.

Will you come for a visit at Christmas?

Love Ruth

"That creep," I said trying to keep my voice down.

"Oh, Ellen, what can we do? Father would just give Ruth a

beating if she told him."

"I think we should show this letter to Amy," I replied.

"But this is our secret."

"I know. But sometimes we have to ask for help. Amy will understand and she will keep your secret."

"I don't know."

Vera finally decided that we should include Amy and later that night we showed Amy the letter.

Amy was not surprised about the news. She just said, "Will it ever end?"

I told both Amy and Vera about my plan to stop this creep.

By the time the evening was over our plan was made. We would be heading to Pearl. We had lots of work to do to get everything organized. Vera and Amy needed to get time off from their jobs. The Hogans had invited me for the Christmas holidays and the Reeses had said I could go so I would be able to go to Pearl without anyone wondering about my visit.

Fortunately, Amy had taken extra money out of my tin that was buried in the backyard. She had done that in the fall before the spot was frozen solid and covered with three feet of snow.

The Reeses were paying for my train ride.

That night only one small cloud graced the sky. It would have to swell up to hold all my thoughts.

Am I the Queen of Secrets? Does everyone have this many?

I stood there watching the cloud stretch out and become bigger and bigger.

Go with the plan, Ellen. Go with the plan.

166

Chapter 18

ON FRIDAY, December 23, Vera and I boarded the train for Pearl. Amy and Martha were to join us in Pearl on the Tuesday after Christmas. They were to go to the back door of the General Store and Vera would make sure that it was not locked. She would have blankets and food there for them.

When I arrived in Pearl late in the night, the Hogans were full of questions for me.

"How is school going?"

"Do you like the city?"

"Are you warm enough?"

"I hope you aren't keeping company with that Connor trash, are you?"

I tried to answer every question but the last one was a problem. If I said yes, they would both be upset. If I said no, that would be a lie.

I decided to answer, "I see her almost every day because she is in the same class at school."

The next day I asked Mamma, "Why can't Martha come home for Christmas? She must be lonely by herself in the city."

"Martha chose to do a very bad thing and we cannot have her in our home anymore."

"Did she get in trouble at church?"

"Yes."

"Did the priest want her to wear a white gown?"

"That's enough child. Some things are just not talked about."

I knew that she would not tell me anymore.

We kept busy preparing for a big Christmas dinner. The Hogans and I would be the only people at the dinner table. I attended Mass with them on Christmas Eve and I tried to keep away from that creepy priest. I saw Vera at church and she said she was ready to carry out the plan.

The next few days seemed to drag on forever. Tuesday night I heard the train whistle blow. I hoped that Amy and Martha had arrived safely. I tossed and turned in my bed. At six in the morning, I rose and quietly left the house. It was very dark yet as the sun did not rise until after eight. I hurried over to the General Store.

Vera, Amy and Martha were all there.

"Is everyone ready?" I asked.

"Yes," came the reply from each of the girls.

Amy carried a knife, Martha had a rope and Vera had a rag. We left for the priest's office.

We all barged into his office and found him in his bedroom. All the better for us.

We marched into his bedroom and Amy demanded, "You miserable creep, take off all your clothes."

He tried to fight us but we held him down while Vera took the rag and stuffed it in his mouth.

Father George was in long johns. This was underwear that was all in one piece from top to bottom. It was obvious that he was not going to cooperate. They managed to get the buttons undone and pull the sleeves off and then pull the long johns down to his knees. They forced him in a chair and Martha and Vera tied him up. Amy held the knife to his throat and then proceeded to move it down to his groin area.

"How does it feel to be on the receiving end, you big creep?

"This is for Martha, Vera, Ellen, Ruth, Betsy, me and anyone else that you have ever touched. You miserable creep!"

Martha shouted, "If you ever think of touching anyone of us again, we will be back to finish the job. If you tell who did this to you, we will be back to silence you."

Amy touched his privates with the tip of the knife and said, "Do you understand?"

The priest bobbed his head up and down. There was fear in his eyes.

"Come on girls," I said. "Let's get out of here."

We scurried out of the office and off to the Eastman house.

When we arrived we were all out of breath. We clamoured into the kitchen where Mr. and Mrs. Eastman and Ruth were seated at the kitchen table having breakfast.

Amy spoke directly to Mr. Eastman, "You may want to go over to see your precious priest. He has fondled one too many girls. While you're there, you may want to gather up the white gowns that he insists they wear."

"What have you done?" Mr. Eastman roared.

"We have done the town a big favour," Martha answered. "And don't you shout at us! Adults are supposed to protect their children not put them at the mercy of some creepy priest."

Mr. Eastman was shocked into silence.

"Girls, it is time to leave," Amy said.

Amy and Martha went back to the General Store. They would stay there until it was time to board the train back to Regina. I headed back to the Hogans. Vera and Ruth were left to face the wrath of the Eastmans.

Our work was done here in Pearl.

The sun was rising in the east and a soft fluffy cloud smiled down on me.

It is time to forgive, forget and move on.

Epilogue

THE RESIDENTS of Pearl will never hear of the priest's embarrassment. He knew that he would have to keep his mouth shut, or he would loose his manhood. Mr. Eastman knew but he would not talk about what he saw because his daughters were involved. If the residents of Pearl ever heard about the incident, the Eastman family would be outcasts forever just like the Stover family.

Mrs. Hogan had some personal papers of the Stover family. Among them were two letters. One letter was to T. Eaton & Co. requesting a baby sister and the other was a reply from the company. The first had never been posted and the latter had a used postmark from Pearl and it was in Henry Stover's handwriting. The letters were about Ellen's sister who turned out to be a doll.

Quiet before the storm was an expression that was used to

explain a short peaceful time that dying people enjoyed just before their death.

Amy, Martha and Ellen would take their secrets back to Regina; the Eastman's and the priest would share this one with them.

There was also a written confession by Henry Stover in which he apologized for beating up the priest.

Will Ellen ever come back to Pearl? Will the call of Prairie Pearl be strong enough to bring her home?

Bibliography

Back to Basics by The Reader's Digest Association (Canada) Ltd. 1981

Canadian Family Songbook by The Reader's Digest Association (Canada) Ltd. 1978 — *O Canada*

Children's Fashions 1900 — 1950 As Pictured in Sears Catalogs by JoAnne Olian 2003

Children's Songbook by The Reader's Digest Association (Canada) Ltd.1985 — *Clementine, Camptown Races, I've Been Working on the Railroad*

Echoes of the Past by The Community of Bengough 1974

Everyday Fashions of the Twenties as Pictured in Sears and Other Catalogs by Stella Blum

Family Song Book by The Reader's Digest

Association (Canada) Ltd. 1970 — *I'll Take You Home Again, Kathleen* — Page 198

Family Songbook of Faith and Joy by The Reader's Digest Association (Canada) Ltd. 1975 — *The Little Brown Church in the Vale* — Page 166

Merry Christmas Songbook by The Reader's Digest Association, Inc. 1981

Our Heritage by The Community of Langenburg 1997

The Bessel Tree by Arleen Gray and Verna Brenner 1989

The Chronology of The Descendants of Christof Betke and Rosalie Gernhart by B. Forbau 1994

The First One Hundred Years by Churchbridge History Committee 1980

The World Book Encyclopedia by World Book — Childcraft International, Inc. 1981

— King George V (1917 — 1936)

— *God Save the King* written by Henry Carey in the early 1700's

ISBN 1-41204281-X